"Please, Cole, don't."

Cole laughed softly. "Come on, Libbie. You've been flirting with me all afternoon. Don't get scared and run away now." His arm came back around her shoulders and pulled her against his chest.

Libbie loved the feel of his hard chest against her cheek, but she shook her head and pulled away. "I think we both realize we have a job to do and it's dangerous to get involved in—well, let's call it personalities."

"Let's be honest and call it sexual attraction," Cole said, taking her hand and massaging the knuckles.

"Cole," Libbie insisted, "we're both old enough to know that if you play with matches, you're going to start a fire...."

Dear Reader,

Spellbinders! That's what we're striving for. The editors at Silhouette are determined to capture your imagination and win your heart with every single book we published. Each month, six Special Editions are chosen with *you* in mind.

Our authors are our inspiration. Writers such as Nora Roberts, Tracy Sinclair, Kathleen Eagle, Carole Halston and Linda Howard—to name but a few—are masters at creating endearing characters and heartrending love stories. Their characters are everyday people—just like you and me—whose lives have been touched by love, whose dreams and desires suddenly come true!

So find a cozy, quiet place to read, and create your own special moment with a Silhouette Special Edition.

Sincerely,

The Editors
SILHOUETTE BOOKS

SE-RL-3A

KATE
MERIWETHER
Honorable
Intentions

Silhouette Special Edition

Published by Silhouette Books New York

America's Publisher of Contemporary Romance

For
Raymond, Karen and Chase

SILHOUETTE BOOKS
300 East 42nd St., New York, N.Y. 10017

ISBN: 0-373-09369-1

First Silhouette Books printing March 1987

America's Publisher of Contemporary Romance

Printed in the U.S.A.

KATE MERIWETHER

lives in Texas and is the mother of three sons: a poet, a minister and a yuppie. She reared her sons by herself from their childhood, and she says with motherly pride, "They're bright and witty and the most interesting people I know." The author's literary tastes are varied; she enjoys everything from romance to espionage. She also loves country music and swears that listening to those three-minute tales has sharpened her story-telling skills.

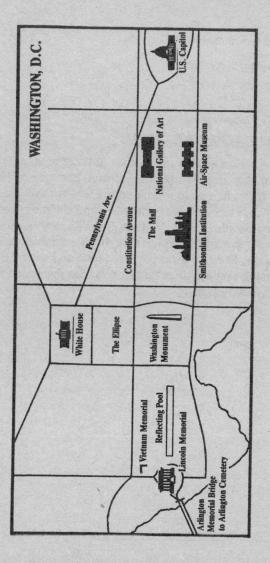

WASHINGTON, D.C.

Pennsylvania Ave.

Constitution Avenue

White House

The Ellipse

Washington Monument

The Mall

National Gallery of Art

Smithsonian Institution

Air-Space Museum

U.S. Capitol

Vietnam Memorial

Reflecting Pool

Lincoln Memorial

Arlington Memorial Bridge to Arlington Cemetery

Chapter One

Libbie Greer jotted a last-minute idea on a yellow legal pad, then stuffed the tablet into a worn briefcase with several bulging manila folders. For some reason she was edgy today, her nerves taut. She was about to make her first major appearance as a professional lobbyist, and she wanted to be sure she looked and performed her best. She took a hairbrush from her desk drawer, ran it through her thick, wavy chestnut-brown hair and made a quick check of her makeup, adding a little lip gloss. Her claret-colored suit emphasized the deep topaz-blue of her eyes. She liked the longer, fuller cut of her skirt, the shorter, nipped-in jacket, and was glad for the trend away from the severe, mannish tailoring of the recent past. She preferred a softer, more feminine look.

Libbie got up from her desk, walked across to the window and watched the rain pour down. November was typically a wet month in Austin, Texas, but why did it have to rain today? The weather might keep people away from the public hearing over at the Sam Houston Building, and she wanted a good crowd; she needed all the moral support she could get. The Pentagon would be sending its best and brightest officers as her opponents, and her experience was no match for theirs.

"I guess I've got everything," Libbie called to Jill Wagner, her colleague and longtime friend, whose office adjoined her own. "Are you ready to go?"

"Be right with you," Jill answered. There was the sound of a briefcase slammed shut, the click of brass latches, then the tap of high heels across the polished wood floor. "Well, you're certainly bright-eyed and bushy-tailed," Jill said in a droll voice. "Why are your cheeks so flushed? Not scared, are you?"

Libbie swallowed hard and managed a faint smile. "Just a little," she admitted. "This is my first time to take the lead, you know. You've done it so often, you've forgotten how beginners get stage-fright and butterflies."

At twenty-eight, Libbie was ten years younger than her seasoned, well-trained supervisor, Jill Wagner, who was the guiding force of an anti-nuclear lobbying group headquartered in Austin. Lately Jill had begun to delegate more responsibility to Libbie, culminating in Libbie's assignment to speak today at a public hearing concerning a nuclear weapons project. They were switching roles, with Jill playing backup to Libbie's lead, and Libbie couldn't help feeling a little apprehensive. Jill was eloquent, persuasive, formidable; Libbie's inexperience might hurt their cause.

"You'll do fine, Libbie," Jill said reassuringly. "You know the facts backward and forward, and your arguments are strong and well reasoned. You'll never be more ready than you are right now."

"I'm not so sure," Libbie muttered, then took a deep breath. Suddenly she felt a jolt of adrenaline surge through her, a boost of confidence. She believed in her cause, didn't she? Then all she had to do was marshal her strength and let the facts speak for themselves. She fished for her car keys, then grabbed her briefcase and umbrella. "Watch out, Pentagon— here we come."

Libbie dropped Jill and their briefcases at the Sam Houston Building, then parked her car a couple of blocks away. The rain had lightened, but she still needed her umbrella. Trying not to bump into anyone, she ran down the sidewalk, hoping her shoes wouldn't be ruined. Ahead of her she saw a military staff car pull up to the curb and drop its passenger, a tall, uniformed officer in a taupe regulation Army trench coat. He must be coming for the hearing today, she thought, trying to catch a closer look. She ran a little faster.

Just as she reached the building entry, closing the distance between them, a gust of wind caught her umbrella and jerked it to the full length of her arm. Thanks to good reflexes, she yanked on the umbrella before it struck the officer's cheek, but in the process she was thrown off balance and stumbled slightly.

He automatically put out an arm to steady her, then glanced down to be sure she was balanced. They were scant inches apart, and Libbie caught his light, masculine scent of musk, rain, and damp wool, the powerful feel of muscle and bone against her shoulders. She lifted her gaze to find a pair of dark, brooding eyes looking at her with surprised interest.

"Thanks," she said. "My shoes are slippery from the wet sidewalk."

"Sure you're okay?" he asked, holding the door open while she struggled to close her umbrella. "I've always thought the umbrella was an underrated invention," he said, giving her a lopsided grin as she fumbled for the catch that would collapse the metal frame. "It's a wonderful weapon, either for offense or defense."

"That sounds like something a soldier would say," she answered pertly.

He whisked off his hat and shook the rain from its brim, then held it against his chest and bowed in a bantering parody of an old-fashioned introduction. "Cole Matthews, United States Army," he said. "At your service, ma'am."

"How gallant," she replied, fighting the urge to bend her knees in a quick curtsy. Instead she offered her slightly damp fingers. "Libbie Greer." Their hands met for only one pulse beat, barely long enough for flesh to touch flesh; yet in that instant they both felt the spark of contact that was something more than physical.

Libbie's lips curved involuntarily in a smile, as though something deep within her felt a sudden gladness that couldn't be restrained. Yet she knew her eyes must have the same puzzled expression she saw in the handsome face towering above her. She fell into step with Cole and walked across the lobby to the elevators. Both of them were now silent, pondering.

A crowd of people, state employees returning from lunch, entered the elevator with them, and they were pushed to opposite ends of the cubicle. To Libbie's surprise, Cole got out on the third floor instead of proceeding to the fifth floor with her. She'd been certain he was with the Pentagon and was here for the public hearing. He paused a moment in the doorway, then smiled as he stepped off. "Watch out for that lethal umbrella," he said. Then he was gone.

The meeting room on the fifth floor was already bustling with activity when Libbie arrived. "Sign here, please," said a pretty young clerk from one of the state agencies, handing her a clipboard listing names, addresses, and telephone numbers.

"They *always* make us sign in for these things," Libbie commented. "Is it so they can keep track of the loyal opposition?"

"Sorry we don't have any glamorous cloak-and-dagger activities," the clerk said, her voice cheerful. "The list is for the Budget and Planning Office, so that we can put you on our mailing list for the future hearings on the nuclear project."

"Well, in that case," Libbie answered, scrawling the requested information before handing back the clipboard. "I certainly wouldn't want to miss one of your announcements."

She entered the small auditorium and joined Jill at a seat near the front, then looked around. There was an easel with a group of charts turned face down, and someone was setting up an overhead projector. There were several men in business suits, doubtless state employees, all engaged in last-minute checks of the sound system or various printed handouts.

"No military?" Libbie commented, still wondering why Cole Matthews had gotten off the elevator on the third floor.

"They'll walk in at precisely one-thirty. Not a minute sooner, not a minute later. That's their style. And everything better be ready for them, or heads will roll." Jill checked her watch and noticed the increased tempo of the support staff, scrambling to finish. "Three minutes to go."

"Hi, there," came a soft West Texas drawl from behind them. They turned to see Dan Williamson, a wiry, middle-aged farmer from the Panhandle who'd reluctantly agreed to come today and express his concerns.

"You're here, Dan! That's great," Libbie said, reaching to give him a welcoming handshake. "I was counting on you."

"Yeah, so you said. But like I told you, Libbie, I've never done any public speaking in my life, not since the day I presented the 4-H award to the high school senior who raised the best calf. I don't know how to write a speech."

"You just be yourself, Dan. That's all that matters." Libbie's smile was reassuring. "We can hire speech writers, but that's not what we need. All we want is your own words saying what you fear will happen if this project goes ahead. Honest doubts from an honest man. That's all."

She squeezed his hand and felt him relax, then took a deep breath to control her own nervousness. She'd been concerned that Dan might not come today. Farmers tended to be reticent and publicity shy, and she knew Dan dreaded being put in the spotlight. Thank goodness he'd put his worry about the nuclear weapon project ahead of his desire to leave the battle to the professionals. Libbie was one of the professionals, but she couldn't do much without a ground swell of public support.

"Drum roll, please," said Jill. "It's one-thirty, and here they come."

The two women discreetly turned their heads to watch the arrival of the military. There were five men, all walking with long steps to the front of the auditorium. Libbie felt her heart skip a beat. Cole Matthews was in the group.

"Wow!" she whispered. "Did you ever see so much brass?" The men were from the Army and Air Force, all in their full-dress uniforms, impeccably groomed.

"Do you recognize any of them?" asked Jill. "The tall one is Cole Matthews. He's been here before—on the MX missile thing, I think it was."

"I ran into him on the elevator just now," Libbie said in an offhand manner. She wasn't ready to make any explanations to Jill. Especially not when she didn't understand herself why she'd felt that strange disturbance when her fingers touched Cole's. Her eyes moved to the man Jill had described as the "tall" one. He stood perhaps a half-inch above the others, but seemed taller with his proud, erect carriage and lithe grace. His skin was darkly tanned, his hair coal-black, his eyes coffee-brown. He'd removed his trench coat. The silver oak cluster on his shoulder indicated that he was a lieutenant colonel, and the ribbons and medals on his chest showed that he'd had a brave, battle-marked career.

"He's gorgeous," Libbie said, unable to take her eyes from him as he nodded at the crowd and took his seat near the easel.

"He's the enemy, and don't you forget it," Jill said. "He's the best officer the Pentagon has for this sort of thing. He'll beat you at your game before you know what's happened, and he'll charm your socks off while he's doing it."

"Charm?"

"Don't tell me you missed that twinkle in his eye. And the lopsided grin."

"How can you tell from here?"

Jill actually blushed. "Maybe you can't see them just now, but believe me, before this hearing is over with, he'll get close enough for you to get the full effect."

"Awesome!" They exchanged smiles.

"Awesome is right. Keep up your guard, Libbie, or you won't be the first green lobbyist to see six months' work go straight down the tubes."

"Should I reverse my collar to hear this confessional? Or are you speaking of an anonymous friend?" Libbie was astounded and eager to know more. Surely it couldn't be Jill Wagner—the cool-eyed professional, the not-to-be-deterred intellectual—who was warning her about this military officer and his devastating effect on women. "Tell me all about it."

"Later. We're here to work, remember? And you're the A-team."

"Welcome, ladies and gentlemen," said a man in a somewhat rumpled gray suit. "Today we're here to solicit public comment in regard to a proposed nuclear project. This involves the construction of an advanced new system for the defense of our country in case of nuclear attack." The man paused and looked at his notes. "Is the public address system working okay?" he asked. "Can you hear me in the back?"

The crowd nodded. They were familiar with the purpose of the meeting and wanted to get on with business.

The man shuffled his note cards again. "Several sites are under consideration, and one of them is located in the Texas Panhandle."

"Yeah, right in my backyard," Dan Williamson muttered under his breath to Libbie. "My farm will be growing glow-in-the-dark wheat if these guys get their way."

The speaker cleared his throat, then continued. "Public hearings will be conducted across the state, as required by law, before an environmental impact statement is released. Recommendations will then be made to Congress and the President by the appropriate agencies. Today is your opportunity to express your concerns so that they can be taken into account when the final decisions are made." He shuffled his papers and put them inside a folder. "Several of you have already signed up to speak today. We'll hear opponents of the project first, and then we'll hear from the military. Please keep your remarks brief, so that everybody will have a chance to talk."

He started toward a seat on the sidelines, then returned to the microphone. "By the way, I'm Bruce Periman with the State Department of Intergovernmental Affairs. My agency is pleased to be the sponsor of today's hearing. Our first scheduled speaker is Molly Barnett."

A heavyset, gray-haired woman in a forest-green pantsuit stepped from the back of the audience and made her way to the microphone. She cleared her throat a couple of times and awkwardly tugged at the hem of her jacket until her eyes found Libbie's. Mrs.

Barnett seemed to relax visibly as she gave Libbie a shaky smile, and she began to speak in a high, breathless voice. "I'm not one to get up in front of a crowd," she said apologetically. "Sure wish I was back home." Her fingers moved restlessly to her throat. "I'll make this short, like the man told us to do."

Libbie nodded encouragement as Mrs. Barnett seemed to falter.

"They want to build more nuclear weapons," Mrs. Barnett said, suddenly lunging forward, eager to get her speech over with. "I just want to tell you that my son was killed in an explosion at a weapons plant. They claim it wasn't a nuclear explosion, and probably it wasn't, or the whole town would've blown sky-high. But there's something wrong with their safety procedures, or my son wouldn't be dead. If they mishandle regular explosives, how can we be sure they won't do the same thing with nuclear stuff? What goes on in those nuclear plants is top secret, and how is anybody ever going to know whether they're operated in a way to protect the workers and the people who live nearby? I don't think they should be allowed to expand until they can prove they'll be accountable for human safety."

She paused and seemed to be staring into space, seeing something no one else could see. For a moment she sagged with the weight of her grief, then forced herself to continue. "My boy is dead. Nothing can bring him back. I'm here today so maybe another mother's son will be spared. That way, my boy won't have died in vain." With a quick nod, Mrs. Barnett turned and left the podium.

"You're off to a good start," Jill whispered to Libbie. "How did you ever talk Mrs. Barnett into coming here today? She's always turned me down."

"Guess I caught her at a weak moment. She was terrific, wasn't she? So much dignity. She wouldn't have been half as effective if she'd cried when she told about her son." Libbie turned to glance around at the audience, trying to gauge their reaction to Molly Barnett's simple plea. Libbie's college training had been in mass communications, the lifeblood of lobbying, and she'd planned today's presentation to be eloquent, emotional, and effective. Jill was right. With Molly Barnett, they were off to a good start.

Dan Williamson spoke next, expressing the concerns of farmers who were afraid nuclear waste would contaminate the soil and water. "The Great Plains is the breadbasket of the world," he said. "How are we going to feed the hungry if our wheat and grain are radioactive? Believe me, if nuclear waste gets into our underground water supply, hundreds of thousands of acres of land will be taken out of production forever. This is serious, folks. Don't let it happen."

Ten or twelve other people spoke, and then it was time for Libbie to wrap up her side's presentation. She sneaked a glance at Cole Matthews and felt even more anxious about the way she'd decided to handle her speech. Would he think she was hopelessly naive and unsophisticated? She'd spent days trying to come up with a persuasive approach, and finally decided to be herself instead of copying Jill's style. It was beyond Libbie's power to be intellectually intimidating, the way Jill was. So far the simple, emotional approach had worked for Libbie, because it came naturally. She still thought it would be better to play to her own

strengths instead of doing a poor imitation of someone else's, but what would Cole Matthews think? She
went to the podium and leaned forward, her brown
curls tumbling across her shoulders, her topaz-blue
eyes warm and sincere.

"Thank you for listening so patiently to our presentation," she said. "We've tried to show you the
real, human concerns so vital to the decisions that will
soon be made. We have all kinds of facts and figures
to back up our position, but we didn't want to bore
you with a bunch of numbers you can read for yourselves. We've got packets printed up with more hard
data than you'll ever want to know, and we'll hand
them out at the end of the hearing today. We chose to
use our time letting real people speak for themselves."

Her soft pink lips formed a smile as she warmed to
her task. "Real people—and weren't they incredible?
A mother, a farmer—people like you and me, ordinary people who'd rather be home at work instead of
here in Austin today. But it's the ordinary people of
this country whose lives are being affected by these issues. And it's the ordinary people who have to speak
out, loudly enough for Washington to hear and respond."

Libbie put away her notes. She didn't need them. It
was time to wrap it up, now, while her audience was
caught up in what she was saying. She dared not let
herself glance in Cole Matthews's direction. Right now
it didn't matter what he thought of her. She was after
votes, and she was never going to win his. He was the
enemy.

"You know, folks, Dan Williamson is a farmer
from Deaf Smith County. The county seat used to

have a slogan pasted on a billboard at the edge of town. It was called 'The Town without a Toothache' because of natural fluoride in the water supply. Dentists there didn't do a whole lot of business, because there was so much natural protection in the water.''

Libbie paused, and let them wonder for a moment where she was headed with her little anecdote. "Ladies and gentlemen, that natural fluoride was beneficial, and nobody cared if it percolated through the soil into the water supply. But radioactive garbage is a different story. If nuclear waste percolates into the water like fluoride did, Dan's home town won't be known as 'The Town without a Toothache.' It'll be known as 'The Town without a Future,' because it'll be dead and buried, right along with the containers of radioactive waste. Let's be sure the Panhandle has a future. Don't let this nuclear project seal its doom. Thank you very much.''

"Wonderful presentation!" said Jill as Libbie hastily took her seat. A group of antinuclear protesters emerged from the back of the auditorium and began to cheer and wave hand-lettered posters. The audience joined in the applause until Bruce Periman made his way to the front and tapped on the microphone, requesting order. "We'll reconvene in ten minutes," he said.

"Glad your part's over?" asked Jill, standing to stretch her legs. "You did a great job, Libbie, just like I knew you would."

"Thanks," Libbie answered, hugging her arms around her body in a gesture of exhilaration. "It doesn't hurt to have a paid band waiting in the wings, though."

Jill laughed. "The antinuke rabble-rousing band, you mean? They never miss a hearing. Be glad they're on your side, because they can be just as noisy if they don't like what you're saying. They can drown out a ten-megaphone sound truck." Jill tucked her briefcase underneath her folding chair. "Come on, I'll introduce you to the opposing forces."

Libbie glanced toward the front of the auditorium. The Pentagon brass were engaged in casual conversation, seemingly oblivious to the warm reception Libbie's team had received from the crowd. "Great," she said, putting aside her folder. "Be sure I get close enough to see the twinkle in his eye."

"Whose eye?"

Libbie smiled. "Don't give me your innocent act. You know who I'm talking about." Unconsciously she fluffed her hair around her shoulders and followed Jill across the room. She saw the group of men turn toward Jill, then felt herself being drawn forward. "Nice to meet you," she said, extending her hand. "Colonel Jackson, Major Dunn. Colonel Matthews and I met in the lobby earlier." She gave Cole a quick nod of her head and he responded in kind. "I'm Libbie Greer, with CNS, the Coalition for Nuclear Sanity. Welcome to Austin."

There was the usual small talk to accompany the introductions, and some good-natured banter between Jill Wagner and the three officers, whom she'd met on previous occasions. On the surface it all seemed cordial enough, yet Libbie was aware intuitively that Cole was giving her his intense scrutiny. It wasn't really in the way he looked at her, with the cursory once-over any man gives an attractive woman. Rather than seeing her with his eyes, Cole seemed to be assessing her total identity and personality with all his senses, with his entire mind and being.

It's like being in a dark cave with an enemy, Libbie thought with discomfiture, and he's not sure whether I'm armed or not. He's trying to decide how dangerous I am. A prickle of uneasiness darted down Libbie's spine, making her stiffen involuntarily. The moment was over almost before it began, and she gave herself a little shake. You're letting your imagination run away with you, she scolded herself. Turn around and look him in the eye.

She turned, quickly enough to catch him before he could mask his searching, unguarded expression. Then, as though nothing out of the ordinary had happened, his eyes twinkled and he gave her a lopsided grin. "Nice presentation, Ms. Greer. It is *Ms.* Greer, I assume." His eyes wandered to her left hand and found it ringless.

"Oh, yes, definitely *Ms.* Greer. I think titles should be neutral, don't you, *Colonel* Matthews? After all, a person's marital status should be irrelevant to her—or *his*—work assignment. Wouldn't you agree?" She gave him her most fetching smile and slowly, deliberately looked at the ring finger of his left hand. It, too, was bare. "However, men still have the advantage," she said in a conspiratorial whisper. "The absence of a wedding ring on a man's finger doesn't necessarily mean the absence of a wife."

He leaned against a column and gave her another crooked smile. "You're absolutely right," he agreed, then waited with interest to find out whether she'd let him get by with that kind of taunt.

She wrinkled her nose at him. So this was what Jill meant by "charm." Colonel Matthews was enjoying his little guessing game—at her expense. Well, Libbie could be coy, too. "Men have so many advantages already," she added. "That's why I decided long ago not to wear a wedding ring."

She'd surprised him. "Oh, so you're married?" he asked, unable to conceal his confusion.

"I didn't say," she said, giving him her most ornery grin.

Bruce Periman tapped on the microphone, calling the audience back to attention. "Let's get started again, folks," he said. "We still have quite a few speakers. At this point I'll turn the program over to Colonel Jackson of the Department of the Army."

Libbie and Jill hurried back to their seats, and Libbie was aware of Cole Matthews's eyes following her all the way across the room.

"What did you think, Libbie? Did you get close enough to see the twinkle?" Jill asked as they scooted into their seats.

Libbie felt heat rising in her cheeks. "The twinkle and the grin, both exactly as promised."

"Uh-oh. You'd better watch out, Libbie. He's big league, all the way. He's absolutely committed to his work, and he'll seize any advantage he can get his hands on."

"Does that include small-town lobbyists?" Libbie whispered, her curiosity aroused.

"He eats little girls like us for breakfast." Jill gave Libbie a searching glance. "You'll have more contact with him in the future because of these hearings, but remember what I told you, Libbie: keep up your guard, or all your hard work will have been for nothing."

"That sounds like the voice of experience," Libbie said.

"No, not quite. Fortunately, I caught on in time." Jill put her hand on Libbie's arm and gave her a quick squeeze. "He's a zealot, Libbie, dedicated to the battle against totalitarianism. I've never met anybody like him before. He's one of those rare souls who are willing to die for what they believe in. He'll fight to his last breath. It's not games and fancy words with him."

Libbie looked across the room at Cole, leaning back in his chair with his arms folded across his chest, one leg crossed over the other. Even at this distance she could feel the sizzling intensity, the barely caged raw power emanating from him. His head turned, as though he felt her eyes on him. Their glances met, held. He nodded and gave her an almost imperceptible wink. Then he turned away. She could see only the side of his face, but somehow she knew the lopsided grin was back on his lips.

Chapter Two

Colonel Jackson, a trim, silver-haired Army officer, took the podium long enough to make a few introductory comments before turning over the presentation to Cole Matthews. "I'm sure you'll find Colonel Matthews's remarks worthwhile," Colonel Jackson said, giving a terse smile to his colleague. "Let me just add that he has had a distinguished career with the Army. Unlike the other staff officers who are here today, Colonel Matthews didn't attend West Point or the Air Force Academy. He worked his way up through the ranks, beginning as a buck private in the Army. He's now on special assignment with the Pentagon, and travels to NATO, SEATO, the Falklands, and any place in between. Please make him welcome."

There was a smattering of applause, and Libbie turned to Jill with raised eyebrows. "He worked his way up from a buck private? I didn't know that was possible."

"Only for someone with exceptional abilities," Jill replied. "They don't usually introduce him this way. They must be trying to combat that 'ordinary citizen' approach of yours. You know, 'Here's Cole Matthews, folks, just another garden-variety fellow.'"

"From the looks of that fruit salad on his chest, garden-variety *hero* sounds more like it." Libbie was impressed and admitted so to Jill.

"Naturally. You're supposed to be impressed. It's part of his mystique. And it always works. Look at this audience."

Libbie glanced around. The words "buck private" had changed everything. Even the people who were here on the Coalition's behalf were giving Cole their undivided attention. "That's the good old USA for you," Libbie said with a rueful chuckle. "How we love underdogs." She turned to Cole Matthews with a new, grudging respect. He'd managed to seize all the warm feelings she'd stirred up in the audience and wrap them around his own cause. He'd just taught her a major lesson: always get the last word. That way you can use your enemy's leftover ammunition.

"Thanks, ladies and gentlemen," Cole said with a boyish smile. "I'm not going to take much of your time, because it's been a long afternoon and I know you're tired of listening. I just want to assure you that the weapons project being discussed today has had top priority and has already been through almost ten years of intensive study. The military has worked hard to design a system that will have the smallest environmental impact, yet at the same time the greatest potential to defend our country against a surprise nuclear attack.''

Cole leaned casually against the podium, deliberately downplaying any sense of urgency. His manner was calm, reassuring. ''I think you'll be interested to know some of the criteria we used. For instance, we had to design a system that wouldn't be obsolete before it was finished. We've had to look at population density and agricultural impact. We've had to exclude locations where the bedrock and water are less than fifty feet deep.''

Libbie turned to exchange a dour glance with Dan Williamson, the farmer who sat behind her. Cole's remarks were undermining the concern that Dan had expressed earlier, making it sound as though the Pentagon had thought of the farmers' objections and worked out a solution. From Libbie's perspective, it was an unsatisfactory solution, but Cole made it sound not only feasible but inevitable. She frowned, then returned her attention to Cole.

''We've had to find a place at least two hundred miles from coastlines and borders to avoid the possibility of radar-jamming by an enemy nation,'' Cole continued. ''We've even had to avoid locations where there are endangered species. For example, we've eliminated seven locations from consideration to protect an endangered cactus.''

There was a snicker of laughter from the audience at the mention of the cactus. Then an angry voice from the back of the room called out, ''What about the endangered species known as *Homo sapiens*?''

''Yeah,'' cried someone else. ''Suppose you build this system and something goes wrong? What if an enemy manages to launch enough weapons to strike the whole system simultaneously?''

A hush fell over the room. It was the terror of the modern world, now framed in one unavoidable question.

Cole leaned forward and gripped the podium. "I have to be honest with you," he said. "There's only one answer to your question. If the entire system were hit at one time, there would be total destruction of the surrounding area."

A wave of frightened whispers swept through the auditorium. No one had expected the military to be so blunt. No one wanted to hear this disclosure. It was too horrifying.

The antinuclear protesters at the back of the room suddenly began to shout and surged forward, heckling and waving their hand-lettered signs until Cole was unable to carry on his remarks. He stood at loose attention, as if he'd expected this to happen and had already planned his response. Then, as though he'd allotted a specific amount of time to the protest and it had now expired, he held up one hand and said very softly, "Now, if I may continue."

The protesters persisted with their jeers, but someone in the audience stood and said, "Sit down and let the man have his say. This is still America, isn't it?''

Somewhat abashed, the protesters went back to the sidelines. Free speech was what it was all about—even for their despised military opponents.

Cole waited until the room was completely silent, then walked to the easel and flipped over the charts. "I told you about the destruction to the surrounding area if the entire system is hit at one time," he said. "But you didn't ask the next logical question, which is,

What if we *don't* build this defense system?" He pointed at the charts, with their diagrams of weapons and missiles. "This is our existing system," he said. "As you can see, it doesn't begin to compare in size or number with that of the other major power. If an enemy should launch a first strike *today*, over ninety percent of our entire defense system would be destroyed. The advantage of the proposed system is that each of our new weapons would require a hit by at least twenty enemy warheads before it would be disabled. It's virtually impossible for any country to launch that many warheads simultaneously."

Cole paused and assessed the audience. Some of the tension had relaxed. "Our present system has become vulnerable. Ladies and gentlemen, we at the Pentagon want the same thing you do—a safe, sane society. But the old lesson of history is that the price of freedom is eternal vigilance. The United States military is committed to the kind of vigilance that will guarantee freedom, not only for American citizens but also for any other nation that treasures peace, security, and self-determination."

He's really good at this, Libbie thought. I bet he's given this speech a hundred times before, but he makes it sound like it's brand-new. I don't think he could do that if he didn't really believe in what he's saying. What did Jill say earlier? That it isn't games and fancy words with Cole, that he'd die for what he believes in? Yes, I believe he would. It's not just his sincerity; it's his commitment. It shows.

Not until that moment did Cole turn to Libbie and give her his full attention, as though they were alone in the crowded room. "Please look at the materials in the handout we've prepared and read them with an open mind," he said. "I think you'll agree that we have a lot more in common than we have separating us. America is still the land of the free and the home of the brave. Let's keep it that way."

Without another word, he quickly turned and left the podium. There was a moment while the audience absorbed what he'd said. Then they broke into loud applause.

Shrugging, Libbie turned to Jill. "How do you call today's game?" she asked. "Looks to me like our team's got no runs, no hits—"

"—And the Pentagon has no errors." Jill sighed. "Damn that man. He's unbeatable."

"Yeah. For a minute there he even had *me* agreeing with him." She turned to look across the room at Cole, her face reflective. "You know, he was amazing when the antinuke crowd started that demonstration to protest what he was saying. I've never seen anybody so cool under fire before."

"I guess he learned that in Vietnam. He was a Green Beret, you know."

"A Green Beret?" Libbie was too surprised to say more. She turned and gave Cole a close look. It was difficult to reconcile the sight of the man in the resplendent, immaculate uniform with her mental picture of a dirty, sweat-soaked jungle fighter. "He doesn't look old enough to have been a Green Beret."

"The rumor is that he quit school and went into the army when he was seventeen, right in the thick of the Vietnam War." Jill gave Libbie a twisted smile. "He's a legitimate war hero, all right. He was in every major battle for ten years. He didn't leave until Saigon fell."

Libbie exhaled her breath in a low whistle. "Wow! No wonder he knows how to handle a few demonstrators." She stood and reached for her briefcase. "Well, I guess we might as well pass out these brochures—if we can still find anybody who wants one."

"Don't be so glum. After a few days people will forget that special aura Cole Matthews carries with him and be more objective. Then they'll read the brochures and remember what Molly Barnett and Dan Williamson had to say." Jill flipped open her briefcase and nudged her lips into a cheerful smile.

Doing likewise, Libbie said, "I'm glad you can be so philosophical about it."

"Philosophical in a pig's snout," Jill said with a bitter laugh. "Why do you think I wanted you to do the presentation today? I'm tired of getting beaten by Cole Matthews. This old mind and body of mine are punch drunk. Sorry to do it to you, Libbie, but I needed fresh cannon fodder."

Despite the day's disappointment, Libbie gave a musical laugh. "And I thought you were doing me a big favor!"

"Well, in a way I was. At least you got to meet the most gorgeous man on three continents."

"Four."

Jill looked across the room and saw Cole Matthews engaged in earnest conversation with one of the anti-nuke protesters. "Maybe you're right," she answered. "Come on, let's hand out our brochures and get out of here. I'll buy you the biggest margarita at Jorge's and we'll salve our wounds."

Cole Matthews was still busy talking to people from the audience when he saw Libbie and Jill shut their empty briefcases and make their departure. He started to excuse himself to catch up with them, then thought better of it. Libbie hadn't given him so much as a parting glance. She must be nursing a grudge. He'd let her stew while he tried to decide on his next move.

State employees came to get the overhead projector and pack away the microphones and sound equipment. Eventually the auditorium cleared, and Cole's colleagues joined him to gather up their charts and leftover brochures.

"Nice job, Cole," said Colonel Jackson with his usual tight-lipped smile. "I didn't mean to throw you a curve by mentioning your background. It just suddenly seemed to me that this was the kind of audience that would appreciate a self-made man."

An Academy elitist, it was hard for Colonel Jackson to admit that an O.C.S. graduate like Cole could go eyeball-to-eyeball with one of West Point's finest. Yet he'd worked with Cole for several years now and had learned to appreciate the man's extraordinary caliber. Colonel Jackson had even wondered if Cole might not be a brigadier general, instead of a lieutenant colonel, if he'd had the advantage of West Point.

Cole shrugged and stuck his ball-point pen back in his inside breast pocket. "We needed to pull out all the stops today. I wouldn't have cared if you'd talked about my Cherokee great-grandmother and her trip to Oklahoma on the Trail of Tears."

Colonel Jackson lifted his eyebrow. "You weren't in that tight a corner, were you?"

"The hell I wasn't. Didn't you see the way that blue-eyed beauty with her sweet smile and warm voice had the audience wrapped in the palm of her hand?"

"Naturally, I did, but—"

"Pure dynamite, and she didn't even realize it. I wonder where Jill stumbled onto someone like her. Libbie Greer is entirely different from the tony intellectuals who usually do these presentations.'' Cole jingled the change in his pockets in a most unmilitary gesture. ''Now, Jill Wagner and her type, I know how to handle. More numbers and better charts. But plain, simple emotion and the common touch like Libbie Greer used—that's a different ball game. I'm going to have to come up with a brand-new game plan.''

''Oh, hell, Cole, you're exaggerating.'' Colonel Jackson reached into his pocket for a cigarette. He flicked open his lighter, then took a deep drag.

''Those things are going to kill you,'' Cole said, as usual.

Colonel Jackson took another pull from the cigarette, then exhaled. ''Not if Ho Chi Minh and three years in a POW camp couldn't get me. I'm too tough to kill.''

Cole grinned. ''I'll agree you're a tough old buzzard. Fact is, your hide has gotten too thick for this work. You're going to have to ask for some R&R with NATO.''

The tips of Colonel Jackson's ears turned red. ''What do you mean by that remark?''

''No offense, Colonel, but Libbie Greer worked this audience like a high-school cheerleader the night before the big game, and you didn't even bat an eye. Your reflexes are gone, man.''

The Colonel stubbed out his precious cigarette. ''Now, just a minute, Cole. *You're* the one the audience applauded the loudest.''

''Sure. But tomorrow morning, when they're back home in Lazbuddie and Quitaque, which one of us will they remember? I assure you, it won't be my fancy charts and razzle-dazzle uniform they'll think about.

It's going to be that all-American homecoming queen with her heart on her sleeve."

Colonel Jackson frowned. "You really think she came across that well?" Maybe it *was* time for him to take a little R&R. But not with NATO, God forbid, not Paris in the winter."

"I know so. The Jill Wagners of the world make a big mistake when they try to sell their ideas intellectually. Libbie Greer knows instinctively that you can never win the mind until you first win the heart. She's going to be one hell of an opponent."

The colonel mulled over the dilemma. "In that case—"

"In that case, we'd better check with the staff assistant who has the sign-in sheets and get Libbie's phone number. I'm going to have to try to see her before I go back to Washington."

The two men exchanged a look. The colonel gave his tight-lipped smile. "Duty before pleasure, I always say."

"Right, duty first." Cole grinned. "Some lucky officers get three years in a POW camp. Me, I'm stuck with a small-town lobbyist. That's the breaks."

The telephone was ringing when Libbie returned home around ten o'clock, feeling better with a tasty Mexican dinner in her stomach and the warmth of tequila in her veins. She'd shared a final toast with Jill, exclaiming, "Down but not out! Tomorrow's a new day!"

Now Libbie was tired and ready for a hot bath and a good night's sleep. She answered the phone with some trepidation, hoping it wasn't someone wanting to discuss today's hearing. She wasn't in the mood for any more shop talk tonight.

"Yes?" she answered, her voice a little cranky.

"Miss Greer—excuse me—*Ms.* Greer?"

There was no mistaking the baritone on the other end of the line. Libbie sat bolt upright in the chair beside her bed. "This is an unlisted number," she said. "How did you get it, Colonel Matthews?"

She could sense the lopsided grin when he answered. "I put the CIA to work on it. Told them it was urgent. Where have you been since six o'clock?"

"Seems like the CIA could've gotten that information, too." The tequila was doing funny things to her body. Her knees felt limp, and Libbie suspected she'd better not try to stand. And there was that weird little prickle up and down her backbone. "What's urgent enough to drag in the CIA?" she asked, a sudden breathlessness in her voice.

"Oh, we always tell them everything's urgent," Cole replied. "They've been looking all over Austin for you. I gave them your description, too. Don't know how they missed you."

"Maybe your description wasn't accurate." There was a tightening in Libbie's midsection. This was a new game, with an expert, and it abounded in flirtation.

"Let me check the card," Cole said, pausing. When he began speaking again, his voice was like warm syrup flowing into her ear. "Age twenty-seven or twenty-eight, height five feet seven inches, weight one eighteen, brown hair, blue eyes, sensational legs—"

Libbie smiled. "That's me, all right. You left off the part about the great figure."

"You didn't let me finish."

"And my fantastic personality."

"That, too."

"And that I'm irresistible to men."

"Of all ages."

"Wow, do you want to be president of my fan club?"

"No, I just want to see you again. Soon." The current that surged between them had nothing to do with electricity and telephone wires.

Libbie gave in to the impulse to push their flirtation game to its limit. "I was just getting ready for bed. What did you have in mind?"

There was a stunned silence, followed by a spontaneous chuckle. "I have some work to finish up tonight. What about breakfast?"

Libbie's merry laughter rippled across the telephone line. "That sound delightful."

"Libbie?"

"Yes?"

"Tell Jill you'll be late getting to the office."

"Oh, I can't do—"

"Libbie."

Libbie caught the crisp note of command in his voice, the tone of a man who was used to having his instructions obeyed without question. Still, she wasn't one of his soldiers. She argued, more for the sake of argument than anything else. And to see how he'd respond. "I have work—"

"*We* have work. We need to talk about this nuclear project. I want to know more about your side's position. We'll need some time." There was no request, no wheedling, only a firm statement. "I'll pick you up at eight a.m."

She couldn't let him have the last word. "Did the CIA get my home address for you, too?" Without waiting for his response, she replaced the receiver and went to draw her bath water. There was an irrepressible grin on her lips.

The rain had stopped, leaving the November day pleasantly cool, perfect for the open-air patio at Sweetish Hill, a popular Austin café. A nosegay of fresh asters and daisies—lavender, yellow and white—decorated the small round table where Libbie sat with Cole. A straw basket lined with a fresh linen napkin contained a variety of breads and rolls for sampling while they waited for their meal to be served. Libbie leaned against the brick wall and enjoyed the warm sunshine on her hair, the rich Colombian coffee in her cup, the dark-eyed male across from her.

"Be sure to try the whole-wheat bread," she said. "It's marvelous, especially with a little of this apple-quince jelly."

Cole peered into the basket and took his time making a selection. "I've got a weakness for croissants," he said. "What kind is this?"

"Cinnamon-almond. Go ahead, take it, and leave the delicious whole-wheat bread for me. The Sweetish Hill bakery is famous for their croissants." Libbie watched as Cole broke off a piece of the crusty roll and sniffed its warm, fragrant glaze before popping it into his mouth. His eyes closed, his lips curled into a smile, as though he were sampling manna from heaven. "You have quite a sweet tooth, don't you?"

"I certainly do," he retorted. "It's my only vice." He favored her with his crooked grin. "Or at least the only one that shows in public." He took another bite.

"Why did I order an omelette? I should've ordered a dozen of these rolls instead."

"Order a dozen and take them with you," Libbie suggested.

"There's not much point in it. I'm going back to Washington long enough to pick up a clean uniform and an attaché case, and then I'm headed for Paris. I'll stuff myself on croissants while I'm there. I always do."

"There must be some interesting perks to a job at the Pentagon," Libbie said, her blue eyes thoughtful. "Like glamorous trips to Paris."

"Glamorous? I never thought of it that way before." Cole finished off his croissant and looked for another. "I'll have an attaché case handcuffed to my wrist and four armed guards from the plane to NATO headquarters. My orders read for me to die before I let anyone take that briefcase from me."

"How can you be so casual when you say something like that?" Libbie asked. "It sounds frightening."

He shrugged. "You get used to it. When you've faced death often enough, you finally realize it's not the worst thing that can happen to you." Their conversation was becoming too serious for such a balmy morning. He grinned at her. "And it does make you appreciate croissants, no matter where you happen to find them."

Libbie was not to be so easily deterred. All her energy was directed to the goal of world peace, and it disconcerted her for someone to show tolerance for the notion of armed guards and orders to die before surrendering a briefcase. "How can you say death isn't the worst thing that can happen to someone? That's a prehistoric military attitude if I ever heard one, to consider human beings expendable. That must be how you countenance this—this nuclear *juggernaut* you're proposing!"

Her eyes were blazing with indignation. Cole reached out to touch her hand. "Whoa, there," he said, as though he were trying to calm a skittish colt. "Don't you think there are things worse than death?"

"No!" Libbie exclaimed. But the expression in his eyes puzzled her. "And you don't either, not if you're honest with yourself."

His large, sun-darkened hand closed over her palm and gripped it. "You haven't seen much of the world if you can make a statement like that and think it's true," he said, his words flat and cold. "Death is better than slow starvation, it's better than agonizing physical pain, it's better than cowardice and loss of honor or love—" His eyes found hers and clung. She could see an old pain buried there before he collected himself and hid it from view. "It's better than the loss of freedom," he continued, his voice and expression now under control. "And that's why we have to have a defense system that will guarantee our nation's sovereignty, even if there are risks involved."

Before Cole could steer the discussion back into his intended route, their waiter arrived with puffy omelettes, crisp bacon, and fresh-squeezed orange juice. "Can I get you anything else?" asked the friendly waiter. "A little more fresh coffee?" He gave them a cheerful smile and brought a steaming pitcher to refill their cups. By the time everything was served, the tension had eased. Libbie and Cole once again engaged in desultory small talk, though neither could forget the moment when flint had struck iron and sent sparks flying.

The early-morning crowd began to thin out, and by the time Libbie and Cole were on their third cup of coffee, the patio was nearly empty. The waiter brought the check, accepted Cole's generous tip with a smile, and disappeared.

Cole tilted back his chair. "Well, now what?" he questioned. "We still need to talk."

"Don't you think it's going to be a waste of time?" Libbie answered. "You have your views and I have mine. Neither of us is going to change."

"Change isn't what I had in mind." The chair dropped forward with a slight thud. "I was thinking of something more in the nature of understanding. I'd like to understand your position. I'd like for you to understand mine. Frankly, we have some similar goals."

Libbie arched a delicate eyebrow. "Not that I noticed."

"What about our desire to protect people? We may have different ideas about how to do it, but—"

"But you want to protect the majority by endangering a minority, and somebody has to be concerned about the safety of that minority. That's my job."

"Safety? Is that your main concern?"

The waiter turned to look at them, as though he wondered why they were still seated.

"Cole, we've been here quite a while. Don't you think we should go somewhere else to talk?" Libbie asked.

He grinned at her. "My place or yours?"

Libbie tried to ignore the sudden flutter in her stomach. "You're a stranger in town. What do you consider your place?" she asked.

"I'm staying in the B.O.Q. at Bergstrom Air Force Base."

"B.O.Q.?"

"Bachelor Officer Quarters."

Libbie shook her head, her lips forming the hint of a smile. "It sounds interesting, but hardly the place for a serious discussion."

"I'm sure the base commander will make a comfortable office available to us."

Libbie didn't have to think before declining the offer with a quick headshake. She didn't intend to go onto enemy turf for an important meeting. "Why not come to my office at the Coalition? It's not far from here."

"Is it still on Seventh Street? I've been over there a time or two." Cole was no more willing than Libbie to set foot on enemy territory. "You're in that remodeled house. As I recall, you can hear every word that's said in every office."

"Not if you talk softly."

Cole noted her squared chin and felt his own. "I'm not so sure the discussion won't get heated at times." They were going to have to find a neutral place. "You want to go walk around Zilker Park?"

Libbie considered the weather. "There'll be lots of runners out on a day like this. I guess they can dodge us."

"The chauffeur can drive alongside and honk to warn us before anybody runs into us."

"Oh, I'd forgotten about the chauffeur. He must be bored out of his mind, sitting in the car waiting for us." Libbie quickly stood, and Cole got to his feet as well. "I suppose he could drop us at my apartment and come back later."

Cole placed an arm behind Libbie's back, guiding her across the patio and out of the restaurant. When he spoke, his voice had a new gruffness. "We'd better forget your apartment until another trip," he said reluctantly. "We have serious work to do today."

They walked underneath a canopy of oak and pecan trees to the bakery portion of the establishment, only a few steps away. "Just a minute," Libbie said, darting in the bakery door and instructing Cole to wait for her. "I'm going to buy a couple of croissants for the chauffeur. He deserves something for his long wait." She emerged with two white paper sacks, one for the chauffeur, the other for Cole. "Here, two new kinds," she said, handing him one of the sacks. "Strawberry and chocolate. You can munch them on the plane when you go back to Washington."

Cole opened the bag and grinned in delight. "You really know the way to break down a man's defenses, don't you?" He reached into the sack, withdrew one of the croissants, and took a large bite. "Umm, delicious," he said, leaning against a tree trunk.

"How do you keep from getting fat, the way you eat?" Libbie asked in amazement.

"I've done my share of eating nothing but rice and beetles for months at a time. Now I can eat anything and never gain an ounce." He took another bite, then tried to brush away the powdered sugar that drifted across his lips. "Besides, I work out every day. The Army insists on physical fitness, you know."

"Let me help you," Libbie said, smiling at the combination of powder-spattered lips and immaculate uniform. Fighting an impulse to kiss away the sugar, she found a clean tissue and reached to blot it away. Cole's cheek was warm and tanned against her fingers, his lips full and sensuous. She and Cole were standing so close that she caught the scent of his light cologne, of soap and shaving cream. Her fingers halted, then traced the outline of his lips. His mouth found the palm of her hand and brushed a kiss in its dark hollow.

"Libbie." It was a murmur of desire.

She felt herself flowing toward him and lowered her lashes, afraid to meet Cole's gaze, lest he discover the powerful feelings he'd aroused in her. In another instant their lips would meet, here, underneath the live oak trees that sheltered the bakery. She could see the rugged grooves in the bark of the tree behind Cole's head, the green leaves threaded with tiny veins. A lady bug crawled up the trunk, oblivious to the pulsing human bodies only inches away. Libbie's hearing became so acute she could hear wind rustling the grass at her feet. Overhead a mockingbird trilled and was answered by the sharp whistle of a cardinal. Libbie lifted her eyes. Cole's face was close-shaven, and she could see the pores of his skin, the tiny sun lines crinkling the corners of his eyelids. The dark hairs that formed his eyebrows were silky-smooth, his lashes short, black, thick. "Your eyes are so dark," she whispered, leaning against his hard, muscular shoulder.

"Indian," he answered through a tight throat. "My great-great-grandmother. A Cherokee." His fingers closed over Libbie's, still at his lips. His eyes raked her face. Her cheekbones were high, her bone structure elegant. The beautiful flush that heightened her color had nothing to do with cosmetics. Her hair cascaded in loose curls to her shoulders, thick and silky and shiny, and he wanted to seize a handful and draw it to his lips. And those incredible eyes, so blue, yet flecked with green in their topaz depths, the pupils dilated, even here in the sunshine, because she thrummed with the same desire that rocked Cole.

He cleared his throat. He had an assignment. He mustn't kiss her. It would ruin everything. "Indian," he repeated, pulling himself to his full height and withdrawing, ever so slightly, but enough to break the magnetism, enough to warn her he was doing it deliberately.

"Indian?" Libbie's voice lifted in a question that had nothing to do with his ancestry.

"Way back. Not much Indian blood left in me, just enough for the dark eyes and hair." He forced his voice to sound matter of fact.

Cole's sudden withdrawal smacked of rejection— rejection similar to something Libbie had experienced in the past. She felt a quickening of the old wound, the old hurt, and wanted to retaliate. "And maybe the warlike tendencies?"

"Warlike? Because I'm a soldier?" Cole shook his head. "My grandmother's grandmother made the march from Georgia to Indian Territory on the Trail of Tears because her people lost a war." There was a sudden, unexpected savagery in his next words. "And my country lost a war, and I've walked my own Trail of Tears. But never again, not as long as there's breath in my body." Cole turned and pounded the tree trunk with his fist. "We've got to defend our country, Libbie. It's your job, just as much as it's mine. Now, where are we going to go to talk about it?"

She let out a long, shuddering breath. She didn't understand this man who stood so close to her yet seemed so far away—who was full of such raging intensity yet had such ironclad control. He almost frightened her. "I don't know," she whispered.

Chapter Three

Cole tucked Libbie's arm in his and steered her toward the staff car waiting across the street from the Sweetish Hill café. It was as though the past five minutes had never happened. Now he was all business. "How much do you know about the environmental impact study?" he asked.

"I've analyzed the documents that were available," Libbie answered, trying to match his professional attitude. "And I've made trips to the site and talked to the people there who'll be affected by the project. Have you?"

"I've been to the proposed site, of course."

"But have you talked to the people who live there?"

"I heard them yesterday. At the hearing."

Libbie's brow furrowed. "Then you don't know a fraction of how they really feel. They're not used to speaking in public, so they were inhibited yesterday.

You need to visit their homes and farms to get the true picture."

The chauffeur, an Air Force enlisted man in a blue uniform, saw them coming across the street and hurriedly opened the rear door for them, standing at stiff attention. He acted surprised when Libbie shoved a paper sack into his white-gloved hands.

"These are for you," she said with a friendly smile. "Thank you for being so patient."

The enlisted man saluted, as if he didn't know what else to do. When his passengers were seated, he slammed the door and started the engine on the staff car. "Where to, sir?"

Intent on their conversation, Cole turned to Libbie, the chauffeur's inquiry unheeded. "You never answered the question I asked earlier. Is safety your primary concern?"

"It's not my only concern, but it's a major one, yes," she answered, noting that the driver was staring straight ahead. The car would not move until Cole gave the order, and the driver would never presume to ask a second time where to take them. Phoenix could freeze over, and we'll still be sitting here, Libbie thought. She felt a giggle rising at the back of her throat and fought it down.

She'd had enough tension for one day. She was ready to go back to work and let Cole Matthews do the same. There was nothing to be gained from any further discussion except frayed nerves. "I suggest that when the time permits, you make a trip to the Panhandle and talk with the people there. Really talk to them, I mean, not just listen to an abbreviated story like you heard yesterday. And then the next time vou're in Austin, we can get together and talk some more." She glanced at the driver and wondered whether she dared give him the Coalition's address, or whether he'd respond only to Cole's order. "I think we've gone as far as we can go for right now."

A trace of a smile brightened Cole's face. "Was that pun intended?" he asked. He had himself under control, but it wouldn't take much for him to reach out and pull her into his arms. The safest thing to do in a situation like this, he'd learned long ago, was mock the physical attraction, ridicule it until it slunk away. Cole retreated into teasing banter, and they both relaxed.

Libbie smiled. "Pun intended." It was a lie, but it was the safest thing to say under the circumstances.

"Let me make another suggestion, then," Cole responded. "You want me to talk to the people in the Panhandle, and I'll be glad to do that." He looked at his watch. He didn't have to be in Washington until noon tomorrow. He'd be cutting his time a little close, but... "There should be a courier plane going from Bergstrom AFB up to the Pantex facility near Amarillo. Let's hitch a ride. I'll arrange for a car, and we can talk to some of your people this afternoon. We can be back in Austin tonight, and I'll hop my military flight back to the Capitol." Cole didn't even bother to glance in Libbie's direction to see whether she agreed. "Back to Bergstrom, driver," he said. "Radio ahead and tell them to hold that courier plane for me. Tell them I'll have a civilian passenger, ID Libbie Greer, and ask them to run a quick FBI check so the plane can land with her aboard."

"Yes, sir." The chauffeur reached for the microphone and repeated Cole's instructions as he drove, dodging the traffic.

"Cole, what are you talking about, FBI and all that stuff?"

"Pantex is a top-secret weapons facility. You won't be able to go inside the plant, but I need clearance for the plane to land with you aboard. If I can't get it, we'll land at the civilian airport instead."

"But, Cole—"

"No buts. We haven't got much time."

"Cole, I can't just take a day off and go traipsing around the country without telling Jill. Besides, you don't need me tagging along. *You're* the one who has to talk to these people."

"But I don't know where to find them, so you have to come along and show me where they live. And yes, you can go traipsing around the country on an important project like this. That's why your Coalition is in existence, remember? It's a free trip. The Army will provide your transportation and expenses."

Libbie glanced down at her high-heeled shoes and sheer stockings, her blue wool-crepe dress. The last time she'd stomped across a Panhandle farm, her sturdy walking shoes were caked with so much mud she'd had to throw them away. She turned her head and studied Cole's splendid uniform, his spit polished black shoes. Her lips curved in a smile. He was so damned overbearing when he started barking out orders. But maybe the dashing Army hero was about to get his comeuppance. Libbie settled into the corner of the car, still smirking at the thought of Cole's shoes after he'd trudged through acres of caliche and cow chips. "I'll call Jill from the airport and explain," she said.

"Not necessary," Cole replied. "I took the liberty of calling her early this morning. She already knows you'll be spending the entire day with me."

The small military plane landed at a cordoned-off runway near the Pantex weapons facility and skidded to a stop. "Wait here, Libbie," Cole said as he unfastened his seat belt and stood, stretching his long legs. He waited until the military courier who'd made the trip from Austin with them had deplaned before he loped down the steps to a waiting Jeep.

Libbie watched through the window of the plane as armed guards met the courier and accompanied him to a second vehicle. There was a strange rigidity in the courier's gait, and Libbie realized it was because he was handcuffed to his briefcase. So they really do things like that, she thought bleakly. Cole didn't just make up the story. I wonder if the courier also has orders to die rather than let anyone take the briefcase from him.

The two vehicles sped toward the weapons facility, leaving Libbie in the plane. The crew remained in the cockpit, and two armed guards remained at the plane's exit ramp. This is all very discreet, Libbie thought, but I'm still surrounded by men with guns who wouldn't hesitate to use them if I made a false move.

Cole's Jeep disappeared from view, turning in a different direction from the armored vehicle carrying the courier. It was a considerable distance to the nuclear weapons plant, most of which was underground for security reasons. It was the first time Libbie'd had the opportunity to view the Pantex plant from inside the fence, but it wasn't the first time she'd been at the scene. She remembered a time months before when she'd been part of a group of demonstrators who'd conducted a rally outside the facility. The Pantex plant was frequently the scene of antinuke demonstrations, and it attracted national attention because it was the final assembly point for all nuclear weapons produced in the United States. Candlelight vigils were often held near the plant when it was rumored that nuclear weapons would be moving out by train to other locations.

From time to time, some bold protesters tried to scale the fence, knowing they would be caught, arrested, and imprisoned—as invariably they were. There are all kinds of heroes, Libbie thought. The ones like Cole, military heroes who face their enemy with weapons; and the antinuke activists, political heroes who fight to change public opinion. She sighed. It had always been so clear-cut to her before, our side versus their side. Now Cole Matthews had come along and shaken her political equilibrium, and the whole nuclear issue was becoming hopelessly complicated. After all, he was just as sincere in his beliefs as she was—

Wait a minute, Libbie thought. Isn't this exactly what Jill warned you would happen? Didn't Jill say Cole would beat you at your own game and charm your socks off while he was doing it? Didn't Jill say Cole is absolutely committed to what he believes in and will die before he'll back down? Come on, Libbie, she scolded herself. Didn't Jill tell you to watch out or you'd see six months of work go down the tubes? How could you be so naive? This guy is *using* you. He's turning on all his considerable sex appeal to distract you from your goal, and you're blushing and stammering and letting your heart go pitter-patter all the time he's doing it. Libbie's cheeks flamed with embarrassment. One hell of a lobbyist you've turned out to be, she thought. First time out and you're...

Libbie glared out the plane window, lost in resentful thoughts. Thank goodness for this little station break, she thought. It's given me a chance to come to my senses. And as for you, Cole Matthews, she added, two can play this game of yours. Fight fire with fire, my professors used to say. Libbie took her mirror from her purse and freshened her makeup, then rearranged her silky, chestnut-colored hair. She practiced a sexy smile while her eyes sparkled back at her from the mirror. The battle was just beginning.

It was almost an hour before the Jeep returned. "Sorry it took me so long," Cole said. "I wanted the plant manager to give me an overview of the safety procedures they follow here. It took longer than I expected." He smiled at Libbie. "Did you doze off? Your eyes have that sexy, half-asleep look."

Libbie lifted one arm and stretched sensuously, returning Cole's smile. "A little catnap, maybe," she replied, widening her eyes and batting her lashes ever so subtly. She drew a deep breath that filled her lungs and made her blue dress tighten across her breasts. "I'm glad you're back, Cole. It was getting lonely out here." Her lips formed the merest hint of a sultry pout. Take that, you creep, she thought. I'm not a fan of old Marilyn Monroe movies for nothing. She felt an inner glee when she saw a muscle twitch at the corner of Cole's jaw.

He leaned across the seat and reached for his flight bag, stiffening when he accidentally brushed against Libbie's thigh. "We're being bumped from the plane," he said. "The courier has to fly on to another base to pick up some classified documents. He'll be back in about four hours to get us. In the meantime, they've given us a Jeep and a driver. We'll talk to as many people as we can this afternoon and come back again later if we have to." Cole took Libbie's hand and tugged her to her feet. "Let's get rolling."

She made sure to let her hand cling to his a little longer than necessary, her thumb curled around his index finger. "Why do you always have a chauffeur?" she asked in a velvety voice. "Do you realize we've never been alone?"

Cole's finger moved around the band of his collar, as if to loosen it. He stepped out of the way so she could come into the aisle, but Libbie was amused to note that he carefully avoided offering a hand to help her as they made their way out of the plane and down the ramp. *So the brave war hero is running scared,* she thought with a secret sense of triumph. *And we have four hours to bounce around in the back seat of a Jeep.*

Dan Williamson was much more comfortable on his own Panhandle farm than he'd been in front of a microphone in Austin. He was downright loquacious as he gave Cole and Libbie a tour of his property. "Now, you see, these irrigation lines are fed by water wells drilled deep underground," Dan said, gesturing to the wheel-shaped devices on either side of the bumpy path. "The water is pumped up from the wells and piped to the growing wheat plants. If the water gets contaminated by radiation, it'll leach into the soil and also be sprayed onto the crops when the irrigation system is operating. Presto, psychedelic wheat, enough to poison millions of people for many generations. And besides death and radiation sickness, there's the possibility of birth defects, cancer—and who knows what future disease we haven't even experienced yet?''

Cole asked the driver to stop the Jeep, and they got out and walked across the field while Dan demonstrated the entire irrigation process. Dan expressed in his own folksy way a farmer's genuine concern that people be nourished by his food products, not poisoned by them. Libbie caught herself hobbling in the rutted path, her flimsy heels offering inadequate support. She stole a glance at Cole's shoes and saw flecks of reddened earth stuck to them. He paid no attention, however, and covered the area with long strides that soon left Libbie trailing behind.

"Come on, slowpoke," he called over his shoulder with a teasing smile.

"How can you walk so fast on a path like this?" she asked.

"Piece of cake," he retorted, though he paused to let her catch up with him and Dan. "No jungle foliage, no *punji* stake traps or buried grenades. Just miles and miles of open fields and blue sky." His head lifted toward the heavens. "This is a perfect place for a defense system," he said softly. "No enemy could ever approach it without being seen long before their planes arrived. No mountains to hide them from our radar. Just all this wonderful open space. It's beautiful."

Libbie and Dan exchanged glances. "It won't *stay* beautiful if you plant nuclear weapons here instead of grain," Dan said dourly. "Nature intended this land to feed the world, and that's what my family's been doing for three generations. I don't intend to be the one who betrays my heritage." His usual easygoing drawl had become an intense whisper.

Cole paused, silent for a moment, thinking about what Dan had said. "I don't intend to betray *my* heritage, either," he said after a time. "My heritage as a free person in a free country. That's what our democracy is all about. That's what I'm fighting to protect, and we have to have a strong defense system if we're going to succeed."

Libbie noticed a surprised expression on Dan's face, as though it were a new thought to him. No! she cried to herself. Not you, Dan! Don't let Cole win you over with his uncanny knack for taking your own ammunition and using it against you, so that all at once you think he feels exactly the way you do. She realized she'd have to do something immediately to minimize Cole's effect on Dan or she'd lose one of her own best allies.

"Democracy means freedom to choose," Libbie said quickly and forcefully. "Freedom to choose the good and reject the bad. It means the right to be protected from things that can destroy you."

"Well, of course," Cole said, bending over to pick up a clod of dirt, then tossing it at a fence post seventy-five feet away. It hit with a resounding thud that broke the tense silence.

"Good shot," said Dan Williamson.

Cole grinned. "I grew up on a farm in Oklahoma. My dad wouldn't let me learn to shoot a rifle till I learned to chuck rocks without missing the target. I hate to think how many spankings my mama gave me for swiping her fruit jars and setting them on a fence post for target practice." Cole picked up a pebble and aimed, then tossed it at a fence post farther away. The pebble pinged when it hit the barbed wire stapled to the post. "Dead-Eye Matthews, that's me."

From anyone else's lips, the words would've sounded cocky and conceited. What is it about this guy? Libbie wondered. He can tell you about his exploits without seeming egotistical. In fact, he's so modest and boyish that he's absolutely endearing, and you can hardly wait for him to tell you more about the rice and beetles he's eaten, or the bayonets and grenades in the Vietnam jungle. You even want him to tell you about the spanking his mother gave him, because you know darn well she slipped him an extra dish of hot blackberry cobbler to make up for it.

"Come on, Dead-Eye," Libbie said, smiling in spite of herself. "We've got several more farms to look at this afternoon. By the time we leave the Panhandle, your throwing arm will be in such good shape you can try out as a pitcher for the Baltimore Orioles."

"Aren't you going to stop by the house first?" Dan asked. "The missus was counting on you to stay for lunch. She's cooked up black-eyed peas, chicken-fried steak, hot yeast rolls, and I don't know what-all."

"She didn't happen to bake a chocolate cake, did she?" Cole asked, reconsidering the need to make haste.

"She sure did. One of those chocolate layer cakes with lots of pecans in the frosting. And let's see, I think she's got mashed potatoes and cream gravy, and salad and fresh green beans—" Dan paused to remember. "She makes the best chicken-fried steak in the county," he added.

Cole patted his tummy. "Never mind that," he said. "It's the chocolate cake I'm interested in."

Dan chuckled. "I've got quite a sweet tooth myself," he said. "Maybe there'll be a little homemade ice cream to go with it."

Libbie sighed. If she had to waddle back to Austin, it wasn't going to be because she'd ruined the heels on her shoes. Maybe she could take a teensy serving of the vegetables and forego the chocolate cake. She took a deep breath and steeled herself for martyrdom.

Cole flagged the chauffeur, and the Jeep pulled alongside the trio. When Cole offered Libbie his hand so she could climb into the back seat, she leaned against him long enough to whisper, "If you don't watch out, you're going to get fat."

He grinned at her as he swung himself over the side of the Jeep and into the seat next to her. "If I do, I won't be able to run from attractive females."

"Attractive females won't bother to chase you anymore," she answered tartly.

Cole clicked his tongue. "Tsk, tsk. And I always thought they chased me for my dynamic personality. Now you tell me it's because they're after my strong, virile body."

Libbie gave him a calculating glance that was designed to increase his pulse rate. Her eyes made a second, leisurely tour that had a devastating effect on her own heartbeat. She controlled the tremor in her breathing and said in a wry voice. "Your *slim, sinewy* body, the one that thrives on rice and beetles."

"Give me a break," Cole whispered. "A condemned man's last meal, if you will. Tomorrow I go to Paris, where chicken-fried steak is not to be found."

"It's the chocolate cake that puts the magic twinkle in your eyes."

Cole winked at her. "You got it, honey lamb. A chocolate cake, a pitcher of iced tea, and a beautiful, blue-eyed wench beside me. Omar Khayyám never had it any better."

Dan's promise of a Panhandle country feast was made good. Libbie resisted temptation in the form of chocolate cake but yielded to hot yeast rolls with fresh butter and honey. When Cole cast longing glances at Libbie's untouched cake, Mrs. Williamson wrapped it in foil for Cole to take with him, since at the moment he couldn't hold another bite. By the time they made their departure, Libbie longed for a good, old-fashioned nap.

They made brief stops at several nearby properties, and Cole listened intently to the concerns expressed by the farmers who owned them. He offered suggestions and solutions for each problem mentioned, and by the time they got into the Jeep to return to the airstrip, Libbie felt sure he'd scored a lot of points. She'd meant to distract him from his sales pitch with a sensual come-on, but somehow it was difficult to be sexy when she felt so sleepy and lethargic.

"I hope it's not raining again in Austin," she said as they left the Jeep and climbed aboard the waiting courier plane at the Pantex facility. "I'm going to have to run four miles around Zilker Park before I go to bed tonight."

"Why?" asked Cole, turning toward her as he fastened his seat belt.

"Because we've been stuffing ourselves since early this morning," she replied. "And if I get fat, attractive men won't chase me anymore."

"You hardly ate a thing," Cole commented. "Didn't even touch your chocolate cake." As the engines revved up and the plane taxied into position on the runway, he gave her an appreciative once-over. "You'll have a whole passel of guys chasing you all over Zilker." He leaned his head back against the seat and smiled at her. "I'd join them myself if I didn't have to get back to Washington."

Libbie felt an inward lurch that had nothing to do with the jet's takeoff. "I think I'll have myself a nap on the trip back," she said. "That feast at the Williamsons made me sleepy."

"Here," Cole said, raising his arm and putting it around her. "Curl up against my shoulder."

Pinpricks of heat coursed through Libbie everywhere Cole's body made contact with hers. She stiffened and sat upright. "On second thought, I'd better not doze off or I'll never be able to sleep tonight."

Cole laughed softly. "Come on, Libbie. You've been flirting with me all afternoon. Don't get scared and run away now." His arm came back around her shoulder and pulled her head against his chest. "We've finally finished our work for the day. It's time to relax."

Libbie loved the feel of his hardened chest against her cheek, but she shook her head and pulled away. "*You* ran from *me* when you thought I was flirting with you," she said. "I think we both realize we have a job to do and it's dangerous to get involved in—well, let's call it personalities."

"Let's be honest and call it sexual attraction," Cole said, taking her hand and massaging the knuckles. He lifted her hand to his lips and brushed the tip of each finger with a feathery kiss that sent shivers of excitement along each nerve path.

"Don't, Cole," she whispered, trying to withdraw her hand. "We're both old enough to know that if you play with matches, you're going to start a fire."

He tightened his grip on her hand, then lifted the tip of her index finger to his mouth and gently nipped it with his teeth. Slowly, sensually, he repeated the gesture with each finger, and when she tried again to remove her hand, he folded her palm and kissed it, then made tiny circles on it with his tongue.

She felt a warm, melting sensation deep within her. "Please, Cole, don't," she murmured, knowing she should sound definite and forceful instead of soft and yielding but was unable to manage it. She fought to control the rapid thud of her heart and said the first thing that popped into her mind. "Besides, we're enemies, you know."

Cole's fist squeezed her fingers until they ached. With his other hand, he tilted her face toward his. "Look me in the eye and tell me we're enemies," he said harshly. "Tell me we have nothing in common, that we'll never share any of the same goals or dreams. Let me hear you say it."

Libbie flinched from his angry gaze. "We're enemies on this project," she insisted.

His fingers seized a loose coil of her hair and wrapped it around his palm so she couldn't avert her head. When he spoke, he spat out the words like artillery fire. "Listen, little girl, you don't have the faintest idea what an enemy is. A *real* enemy—the kind that'll stop at nothing to kill you or maim you or torture you until you wish for a quick, merciful death. So don't use words you don't understand. It's obscene."

Libbie tried to jerk away her head and felt a sharp pain at the temple where her hair was caught by Cole's fist. "Don't be condescending to me," she retorted. "Don't say *little girl* in that superior tone of voice. I'm a grown woman, and I know what it is to have an enemy. They don't all jump out from the brush and aim a machine gun at you, you know. Sometimes they—they try to seduce you so you can't keep your mind on what you're doing. If you want to talk about something obscene, I think that qualifies!"

"Is that what you think I'm doing?" Cole's handsome face registered surprise.

"I understand that's your favorite strategy," Libbie said, her eyes narrowed in anger. "The one you use against all your female opponents." She paused to take a shaky breath. "I also understand that it works every time. But not with me, *Colonel Matthews*. I'm just as committed to my cause as you are to yours, and I don't intend to let you fasten my scalp to your belt along with all your other battle trophies!"

Cole's fist loosened its hold on her hair, and his fingers stroked the chestnut strands. "But it's such a beautiful scalp," he said. "From the first time I saw you, I wanted to bury my face in that silky hair of yours."

Libbie shook her head, making her curls bounce. "See, there you go again. I'm trying to have a serious discussion with you, and you're still trying to seduce me."

He let go of her hair and leaned into the far corner of his seat, away from her. There was a long, uncomfortable silence. "No, Libbie, you're wrong," Cole said at last. "You're trying to have a serious *argument* with me, not a discussion. I don't want to fight with you, so I'm trying to change the subject. But understand this: there's not going to be any seduction. If anything happens between us, it's going to because you want it to happen just as much as I do."

"You make it sound like it's a *fait accompli*," she grumbled, but she was glad to put an end to the hard feelings that had threatened to get out of hand.

"Ten minutes ago I thought it was," Cole said, laughing, more at himself than at her. "Now you've got me guessing." He turned toward her with a gentle smile and offered his hand. "Truce?"

"Are you going to offer me your greatgrandmother's peace pipe?"

He reached into his hip pocket and pulled out a clean handkerchief. "No, but I'm waving a white flag. Will that do?"

"You'd better keep the white flag," Libbie said, smiling. "You'll need it when you eat the rest of your croissants and that extra piece of chocolate cake." She reached out her hand and accepted his. Their handshake was warm, friendly, only slightly suspicious, slightly erotic. "Truce," she agreed. As an afterthought, she added, "For the time being, anyway."

"I'll be on the alert for the war signals," Cole said, settling down for the remainder of the flight to Austin.

"How will you know?"

"Have you forgotten my ancestors were Indian?" he said. "I'll just watch for smoke from your wigwam. Those eyes of yours could start quite a fire when they shoot off those angry sparks." Cole closed his eyes as though he were going to drift off to sleep. Grinning, he added in a husky undertone, "As a matter of fact, I think you're capable of starting all kinds of fires. And not just with your eyes, either.''

Before Libbie could think of a squelching retort, the copilot left the cabin and came to stand beside Cole's seat with a message. "Sorry, Colonel Matthews," he said. "There's a heavy storm system from Dallas to Austin. We've been ordered to detour the plane and land at a military base in West Texas, well out of the path of the storm."

Cole was instantly alert. "But I have to hop that military flight from Bergstrom back to Washington. It leaves at eight o'clock. How long will we be delayed?"

"I'm not sure, Colonel. Probably several hours. But we can't take any chances with the weather. The courier is carrying top-secret documents. The safety of those documents takes priority over everything else." He handed Cole the radio message. "This isn't an Air Force order, sir. It's straight from the Pentagon."

Chapter Four

Libbie kicked off her shoes, tucked her feet underneath her, and leaned against the corner of the sofa to watch TV while she waited for Cole to return with more information about their flight. Except for a janitor who methodically emptied wastebaskets and ashtrays into a trash cart, she was alone in the B.O.Q. lounge of a West Texas military base. The military courier who'd been on their flight had been whisked off to Security, while she and Cole had been welcomed by an officer from base headquarters who'd done his best to provide for their comfort during the layover.

Libbie smiled at an amusing exchange of insults between the characters in the rerun. They're always so quick with a comeback, she thought with envy. They always have the perfect one-liner to wither the opposition.

Her own experience with the opposition had been considerably less than successful, she thought, reflecting upon the day's events. She'd tried to play the vamp and thereby distract Cole from his objective, but she'd failed to bring it off. Instead it was Cole who'd made her own skin sing with pleasure when his lips had toyed erotically with her hand, causing Libbie to be the one whose attention was diverted. *Jill should never have turned this assignment over to me,* Libbie thought. *She should've done it herself. Cole Matthews wouldn't have broken through Jill's resistance the way he has mine.*

Padded footsteps in the hallway broke her reverie, and Libbie turned her head to see who was coming into the lounge.

"Hi," Cole said, leaning against the doorpost in his stocking feet, his jacket and tie missing. His starched tan poplin Army shirt was tapered to fit like a glove, his trousers snug across the waist and hips. He looked lean and trim with his officers' black stripe running the length of his leg, and even ten feet away, Libbie could tell his abdomen was flat and hard.

She felt a little catch in her breathing. "Hi," she answered. "What's the news?"

"It's going to be at least an hour," Cole said. "There's a bad thunderstorm stretching from Dallas south, and they're afraid of wind shear. Looks like we're grounded for a while." He shoved his hands into his pockets. "What size shoes do you wear?" he asked.

"Seven and a half. Why?"

He grinned at her. "We're in luck, then, if you still want to do a four-mile run before it gets dark. I found a nurse upstairs who's about your size. She has a sweat suit that ought to fit, but I wasn't sure about the shoes."

Libbie glanced at Cole's stockinged feet. "Do you plan to run barefooted?" she asked.

"No. I've been cleaning up my shoes, but the polish needs to set before I buff them. I've borrowed some running gear from one of the young lieutenants." Cole walked across the room and reached out a hand to help Libbie to her feet. "Come on, champ, and see if you can shame an old man who's out of practice."

Cole's palm was warm and firm against Libbie's. She curled her hand into his and fell into step beside him. "What do you have up your sleeve, Colonel Matthews?" she asked. "Aren't you satisfied with beating me twice in two days already?"

He paused in the doorway and smiled down at her. "Item one, I'm not at all sure I've beaten you at anything, yet. Item two, even if I have, I'm a gracious winner. I'll give you a chance to redeem yourself and make a fool out of me."

"And how am I to do that?" Libbie asked.

"I meant it when I said I was out of practice. I haven't done any running since I got out of O.C.S. I just hope my great-grandmother's spirit never finds out I was outrun by a mere girl."

Libbie's foot began to tap in impatience.

Cole held up his hand, realizing almost too late his mistake. "Correction," he said, grinning again as his eyes assaulted her body where the soft blue wool clung to her gentle curves, "I used the wrong term. I hope my great-grandmother's spirit never finds out I was outrun by a lissome young maiden." Cole backed her against the doorjamb and rubbed her nose with his.

Libbie's pulse raced at the nearness of his mouth to hers. If she moved her face the tiniest bit, their lips would touch. A purring started in the back of her throat as Cole drew nearer, and she could feel his breath on her cheek.

The clatter of the trash cart announced the return of the janitor from the adjacent sun porch.

Cole coughed and pulled away. "Go upstairs to room 205," he said to Libbie, coughing again as though he had something caught in his throat. "That's where you'll find the nurse who's going to let you borrow her running clothes. You can change up there."

Libbie turned and glared at the janitor's back. "Is this what's known as being saved by the bell?" she muttered.

Cole rumpled her thick curls. "No," he said, whistling softly through his teeth. "It's what's known as being cheated by a squeaky wheel." He tilted her chin until Libbie's lips softened and curved upward. "You have the most beautiful smile," he said, the words seeming to slip unbidden from him. Then, sighing as though a special moment had been lost, he added, "Let's go. Loser buys the drinks."

Libbie gave him a half-hearted wave and made her way to room 205. She ought to be able to run four miles. She ran at least two miles every day, sometimes more. She even ran in the Austin 10K every year. But never with her heart hammering the way it was right now.

The running track adjoining the golf course and swimming pool was deserted, because it was chow time at the dining hall. The late-afternoon sun was suspended in the western sky like a giant orange disk, bathing the barren West Texas landscape in the brilliant twilight hues of the desert. The sky was indigo, without a single cloud to hint of the ferocious storm that raged between Dallas and Austin.

For the first two miles, Cole ran well ahead of Libbie, but after that, thanks to constant training that had built up her wind and endurance, she began to gain on him. On the last lap she took a deep breath and sprinted past him to the mile mark, then dropped onto the grassy slope beside the track, too exhausted to take another step.

Cole touched the post in symbolic completion of their race, then threw himself down beside her, gasping for breath.

"Did you hold back and let me beat you?" Libbie asked in a suspicious voice.

Cole rolled over onto his stomach and buried his face in the crook of his elbow to wipe away the sweat. His back rose and fell swiftly from his labored breathing, and he shook his head at her. "Let me catch my breath before you start the inquisition," he managed to mutter, some of his words so feeble they were lost in the evening breeze.

"Are you all right?" Libbie asked, a little alarmed. No one should try to run four miles without being in good condition, but it hadn't occurred to Libbie that Cole might not be in shape for their run. He seemed to be a perfect physical specimen.

He continued to gasp. "No, I can't get my breath."

"Cole!" Libbie scrambled to her knees and bent over Cole, grabbing his shoulder to turn him over. "What's wrong?"

"I think you're trying to kill me." He flopped over as she struggled to turn him and gave her an impish grin, then reached out his arms and pulled her down beside him. "I told you I hadn't done any running since I left O.C.S." He took her hand and placed it over his pounding heart. "See what you've done to me? I told you I was an old man, but you wouldn't listen."

"Seems like a perfectly healthy heart to me," Libbie said, feeling the steady pounding underneath her palm. The twilight cast shadows over his features, hiding his expression from Libbie's view, but she could sense the energy coursing through Cole. His hand crept up her back, slowly drawing her toward him, toward his strength, toward that energy that seemed ready to explode into action. Their bodies were so close together that she could feel the dampness in his sweat suit, smell the grass crushed underneath his head. If she made the slightest move, the magnetism between them would erupt with a force as powerful as a volcano.

She lifted her gaze. They were in an open field, treeless and flat as the desert, in full view of anyone who happened to pass by. Nearby were barracks with windows facing in their direction. Libbie took her hand away from Cole's chest and sat up cross-legged beside him. "Just how old of an old man are you?" she asked, straining for normalcy in her voice.

He sat up and leered at her. "Chicken."

She shrugged. "You're damned right. My Scottish great-grandmother always said, Never lose your head—or your virtue—in public."

"She was probably quoting Mary Queen of Scots."

Libbie's silvery laughter was caught and tossed by the wind. "Words spoken by Mary on her way to the executioner's chopping block, no doubt."

"Tell me, Ms. Greer, what did your sweet little granny have to say about losing your virtue in *private*?"

"Oh, she was a very proper Scottish woman. That wasn't a subject she'd discuss with anyone." Libbie dug her fingers into the grass behind her, feeling the moist, cool earth that nourished its roots. "You didn't answer my question," she prodded. "How old are you?"

"Why are you so curious? You make it sound like I'm as old as Methuselah."

"I wasn't curious until you started calling yourself an old man."

"Hasn't anybody ever told you it's not the years, it's the miles?"

Libbie chuckled. "Well, my Scottish granny would consider it rude to ask how many miles you have on your odometer." She hesitated, then added, "But maybe it would be all right to ask about the model year."

"No wonder Mary Queen of Scots lost her head. She probably asked too many impertinent questions, too." Cole stood, then offered Libbie his hand and pulled her to her feet. "I'm thirty-seven. And my odometer has turned over at least three times. I'm no match for a lissome young maiden like you. That's why you beat me in the four-mile run."

Libbie squared her hands on her hips and glowered teasingly at Cole. "I never would've thought you'd be the kind of man to make excuses for his failures," she said with feigned petulance. "Or be such a sore loser you'd take all the pleasure out of my beating you. But I guess when you get old, you get crotchety."

"Is that so? Did you learn that from your Scottish granny, too?" But before Libbie had time to react, Cole grabbed her and pulled her against his chest in a huge bear hug, then lowered his face, searching for her mouth. "Come here," he said gruffly, "and I'll show you what an old man can do. I may not be as fast as I was when I was younger, but I'm a whole lot more thorough."

"Cole, no," Libbie squealed, twisting in his arms and enjoying herself immensely. Just as his mouth found hers, she jerked her head, pulling out of reach. "Don't," she said, squirming while he tried to hold her still. "People will see us."

"Who cares? We don't know anybody here." His hands found her cheeks and held her face in a firm grip. "Now, be still," he ordered. "You're just a babe in arms, and I think I can teach you a trick or two about kissing."

"Uh-oh," Libbie squirmed again, then broke from his grasp. "My granny warned me about lecherous old men."

Cole stalked her. "Did she warn you in specific detail?" he asked. "Do you have any idea what wicked, carnal delights might be performed upon your lush, willing body?"

Libbie backed slowly away, her pulse thrumming, her senses reeling. "Don't you mean *un*willing body?" she asked in a choked voice.

"No, I mean *willing*. Eager, in fact. I can read it in your eyes."

Libbie shook her head. "Maybe so, but this isn't the time or place for us to do anything about it."

Cole uttered an oath. "You're beginning to sound like a broken record."

"Sometimes I'm the one to say it; sometimes you are. And when we do, we're right." She reached for his hand. "Come on, let's go back to the B.O.Q. and see if there's any news about the storm."

Cole gripped her hand until her fingers ached. "One of these days..." he muttered.

"Yeah, I know." For a brief moment, Libbie leaned her head against Cole's shoulder. "Come on. You owe me a drink. Loser buys, remember."

There was a surprised bark of laughter. "I'm not the only loser tonight, Libbie." Cole brightened. "But then, the night's not over yet, is it?"

When it became certain that the storm wouldn't wear itself out before morning, Cole busied himself making other arrangements to get back to Washington. He learned that he could hop a military flight to an air base in Illinois, then switch to a Washington-bound plane, avoiding the Texas storm entirely. Libbie would stay behind and go back to Austin with the courier the following morning.

"The base commander is giving you the VIP suite for the night," Cole told Libbie, one hand over the telephone receiver in the B.O.Q. lounge. "You can have breakfast in the officers' dining room in the morning, and they think the courier plane will be able to leave for Austin by six a.m. A driver will be standing by at Bergstrom to pick you up, so you should make it to work on time."

Libbie nodded in agreement, then asked, "What time does your plane leave?"

Cole glanced automatically at his watch. "Ten-thirty. We have about three hours." He turned his attention to the telephone. "Thanks, Major. Sounds like you've covered everything. Send over a driver so I can take Ms. Greer into town for dinner.... Where do you recommend?... Give us half an hour to shower and change clothes. Thanks." He dropped the receiver into its cradle, then turned to Libbie. "I'd rather spend the next three hours in that VIP suite with you, but I guess your Scottish granny would prefer the Country Barn Steakhouse."

"No doubt Granny would." Libbie wrinkled her nose. "I can just see you and Granny in the VIP bed together."

Cole grinned. "I've always liked older women, the kind with a little experience." He stood and threw an arm casually across Libbie's shoulder, then leaned forward to whisper in her ear, "Tell me, you beautiful, blue-eyed wench, have you had a *little* experience?"

Libbie gave him a cherubic smile and mentally straightened her tilted halo. "That, Colonel Matthews, is for me to know—"

"—And me to find out. And I will. That's a promise." His dark eyes seemed to smolder with pent-up desire. "The VIP room is at the end of the east wing." He pointed her in the proper direction as they left the B.O.Q. lounge. "Leave your dress shoes outside the door, and I'll clean the mud off for you while you're changing clothes."

"But, Cole, that's not necessary," Libbie objected. Fiercely independent, she was appalled at the idea of someone else's performing such a menial task for her. "I can clean them myself."

"Don't argue," Cole said firmly. "I said I'd do it for you. It's no job for someone with soft, pretty hands and long fingernails." He tilted her chin, started to give her a quick kiss, thought better of it and sighed wistfully. "I'm sure we can think of more pleasant tasks for these delicate hands of yours."

"Any suggestions?" Libbie inquired with a merry laugh.

"Don't ask." Cole turned in the opposite direction when they reached the end of the hallway. As Libbie went into the VIP suite, she heard the slow, grudging retreat of his footsteps.

Even on a week night, the Country Barn was crowded. It was a popular restaurant, justifiably famous for its Texas-style mesquite-grilled steaks, individually cut to order according to the thickness indicated by the customer's thumb and forefinger. Libbie and Cole wormed their way past throngs of robust eaters to the only empty booth, one on the far wall, away from the five-piece band and small dance floor.

Insisting that she was still stuffed from the hearty noon meal served by Mrs. Williamson, Libbie ordered only a salad. Cole claimed that running four miles had left him famished, so he ordered a "small" steak, a size described by their waitress as something less than sixteen ounces.

"We're pretty busy tonight," the waitress said. "It's going to be a while before your order's ready. Might as well enjoy the band and have yourselves a spin around the dance floor." She stuck her pencil behind her ear, gave the table a desultory wipe and hurried off to another group.

"All right, you lonesome cowboys," the lead singer spoke into the microphone. "We're going to warm up with one of those oldies but goodies, a Hank Williams tune called 'I'm So Lonesome I Could Cry.' Hit it, fellows." The singer warbled the song in a husky voice that delighted the audience. By the time the waitress returned with Cole and Libbie's drinks, the band had gone into a frolicking version of a current hit that had the crowd in a foot-stomping pandemonium.

"The band's hot tonight," the waitress said, smiling as she slid a mug of draft beer across the table to Cole, then set a frozen margarita in front of Libbie. Libbie's foot was stomping right along with the crowd, and Cole was clapping his hands to the rhythm.

It was too noisy to talk, even when the fiddler tuned up and played a long, mournful solo. When he'd finished, the lead singer announced the Cotton-Eyed Joe, and the high-spirited audience scrambled into place for their favorite dance.

"Come on, Libbie, let's join them."

She gave Cole a stricken look. "I don't know how to do country-and-western dances," she said.

"What kind of Texan are you, anyway?" Cole said, refusing to take no for an answer. He stood and pulled Libbie to her feet, then led her onto the dance floor and positioned her beside him.

"I'm not a Texan, at least not a native," she answered. "I'm originally from California."

"Well, if you're going to live in Texas, it's time you learned how to do kicker dancing," Cole insisted. "It'll be a new experience for you." He put his right arm across Libbie's right shoulder and pulled her left arm around his waist, then lightly linked hands with her. Other couples, ahead of and behind them, took the same position and formed a circle.

"Cole, I'm going to embarrass us," Libbie whispered. "Let's sit and watch until I figure out how to do it."

"Just follow my lead. It's not that hard. Start with your left foot, take quick steps forward and back, then kick."

Cole's brief instructions may have contained an accurate description of the steps involved in the dance, but did no justice at all to the lively caper and quick movements. Guided by his firm biceps at her shoulder and his strong torso against hers, though, Libbie abandoned herself to the dizzying four-four tempo of the music. The dance floor became a kaleidoscope of shifting form and color, teeming with infectious energy and enthusiasm. When the dance ended with a final kick, she dissolved against Cole's chest in helpless laughter.

"Didn't I tell you this was going to be a new experience for you?" he asked, his fingers tousling her silky chestnut hair. The band tuned up for a waltz, a slow number so the dancers could catch their breath and cool off after the boisterous Cotton-Eyed Joe. Cole slipped his arms around Libbie and swept her back onto the dance floor, her head cradled against his shoulder. "So you're from California, huh?" he asked.

She nodded, enjoying the gentle sway of their bodies.

"What brought you to Texas?" Cole was a good dancer with an excellent sense of timing, and he took a long gliding step to the music that lifted Libbie's body closer to his.

She flinched at the question. It had been a long time since she'd let herself think about her reason for coming to Texas. The past, she'd thought, was safely buried. "Oh, the usual," she said in a light voice. "I wanted to get away from home, just like everybody does at eighteen, so I came here to go to college."

"But didn't you want to go back home after you graduated? What about your family?"

"It took me a long time to graduate," Libbie said, groping for words that wouldn't reveal too much. "I had to work my way through. By the time I finished my degree, a lot of things had changed at home, and I was pretty much involved as a volunteer lobbyist in Austin." She burrowed her head into the Army-green wool of his uniform, keeping her lashes down. "You know how it goes. One thing leads to another, and one day you realize you've changed too much to go back to your old life."

"Yeah. I know." Cole's arms pulled her closer. "Why won't you look at me?" he asked. "Am I being too nosy?"

Libbie lifted her eyes, then quickly glanced away. Cole's gaze was too probing to meet head-on. She had the feeling that if he could see her eyes, she wouldn't have to say a word, because he'd be able to stare into her very soul and read every secret hidden there. He seemed to have some kind of intuition that exceeded ordinary awareness. It made her feel vulnerable. "Not nosy," she said softly. "But you're getting close to a raw nerve. Let's talk about something else, okay?"

He gave her a reflective glance. "When people uproot their whole lives, it's usually because a love affair's gone sour."

Libbie's jaw tightened. "Why didn't you ever go back to Oklahoma?" she asked, determined to divert the subject from herself. "Was it because of a broken love affair?"

He stiffened and missed a beat of the waltz, throwing their rhythm off for a moment.

"I'm sorry, Cole," Libbie said, realizing too late that she'd blundered onto his secret just as he'd blundered onto hers. "Forget I ever asked. Tell me about Washington. What's it like to be assigned to the Pentagon?" She slipped her arm a little higher around his neck and managed a smile.

They were at the edge of the dance floor, near their booth. The waltz was almost over. Cole stopped dancing and drew Libbie away from the other dancers. "Excuse me," he said, cutting a path through the crowd. When they got back to their booth, he slid across and picked up his lukewarm beer with fingers that trembled. "Libbie, there are things I don't want to talk about, too," he said after a long, painful silence. "It has nothing to do with you or with the fact that I'm attracted to you."

She nodded and toyed with the plastic stirrer in her now watery margarita.

"I'll tell you this much, and then let's put it behind us, okay?"

"Cole, you don't owe me any explanation. Please, everybody has things he doesn't want to talk about because it hurts too much. Your past belongs to you just like mine belongs to me. Let's leave it that way." She took a sip of her drink. It tasted awful.

He leaned across the table and gripped her hands. "For some reason, I want to tell you part of it. It's strange," he said, shaking his head. "I never talk about it to anybody." His dark eyes scanned the room, then came back to Libbie. "There was a woman. I loved her very much." A deep sigh shuddered through his body. "We got married and had a child. Libbie, I have a daughter. She's thirteen years old."

Libbie felt herself turn cold from shock. "What about your wife?" Libbie couldn't stop herself from asking the question. The word *wife* tore at her.

"We aren't married anymore." Cole turned and craned his neck over his shoulder. "Where's our waitress?" he said, terminating the personal discussion. He turned back to Libbie with a neutral expression on his face. "I'm ready for my steak. If she doesn't hurry up and bring our order, we're not going to have time to eat it."

Confusing emotions swept over Libbie, and she hardly knew how to react to Cole's disclosure. It was so odd to think of him as a once married man, devoted to a wife and daughter. That image battled with the pictures she'd already formed of a warrior on the prowl, a charmer who manipulated women, a gung ho flag waver, a healthy male who could rouse a woman's passions and undoubtedly satisfy them—and a man who could hurt and not be afraid to show it. Libbie's fingers, still gripped in his, turned upward in a gesture of warmth and affection.

"I'm sorry, Cole," she said simply.

He averted his gaze. "Thanks." He took a sip of his beer and made a face. "That stuff tastes terrible," he grumbled. Just then the waitress headed their way with a salad for Libbie and a huge steak that lapped over the edges of the plate for Cole.

"Here you are," the waitress said cheerfully. "Let me bring you a cold beer. I bet that one got warm while you were dancing." She turned to Libbie. "How about you?" she asked.

"Just coffee, thanks." Things were back to normal. The band had begun to play "Blue Eyes Crying in the Rain."

For just a moment Cole's veneer crumbled. "I'll probably never listen to this song again without remembering tonight and thinking of you," he said.

"But I'm not crying," Libbie protested.

"Yes, you are. Your tears don't show, but they're there. I can hear them falling, one silent drop at a time."

"Don't you think everybody weeps for the past at one time or another?"

"I don't know, maybe they do," Cole said. "I never did until tonight."

Their parting kiss would have shocked the pilot and the flight engineer, but after almost fourteen hours of yearning for a kiss that hadn't happened, nothing could stop Cole and Libbie now. He found the most secluded corner of the hangar and pulled Libbie tightly against him until she could hardly breathe. When every curve of her body was molded to his, Cole lifted his forefinger and traced the outline of her eyebrows, then her eyelids, before lowering his head to brush them with his lips. Soft murmurs rose in Libbie's throat, and Cole's mouth made its way to her ear, tracing circles with his tongue, then nibbling at her lobe.

Desire flamed through Libbie, her entire body blazing with urgent demands. She lifted her face for his kiss. Cole's mouth was hot and moist as he coaxed open her lips. Her tongue quivered, sensitive and receptive as it touched his, then began a playful, teasing duel that soon made his breathing ragged.

After checking to be sure they were shrouded in darkness, Cole leaned forward from the hips, nudging Libbie against the wall.

She gasped with pleasure when he cupped her breast, stroking it through the soft wool of her dress. He rocked against her and buried his face in her neck, his lips kissing the sensitive hollow while his hands caressed her breasts. His mouth plunged lower, his teeth nipping, his tongue inflaming her further, and when he began to unfasten her dress, she helped him. They had so little time. She opened the bodice of her dress and his hands slipped inside to free her breasts.

He groaned. "It's so dark in this hangar," he said. "I wish I could see you." He cupped her bare breast and gently caressed it until she was dizzy with wanting more.

"Cole," she whispered, twisting as she drew his face down. When his mouth closed on her nipple, she let her head fall back, sighing with pleasure. "I want you." It was a simple statement of desire. Her hand fumbled in the darkness for his waist and crept downward to caress him.

"Oh, God, Libbie," he uttered in a choked voice. His mouth moved across her body to feast upon her other breast.

Outside on the runway, the jet engines of the military plane began to roar, drowning out the sounds of human passion.

"It's time for your plane to take off," Libbie said, straightening and trying to pull herself out of an emotional daze. Her fingers were clumsy as they struggled with the buttons to her dress, and she thought the roaring in her ears seemed as powerful as that made by the jet engines.

Cole groped at his tie and tucked in his shirttail, then sagged against the hangar wall, trying to control his rapid breathing. He pulled Libbie against his chest so he could speak into her ear and make himself heard above the engines. "Guess I ought to turn in my Good Conduct Medal," he said. "I shouldn't have let things get out of hand."

Libbie shook her head. "It wasn't your fault."

"I feel like I ought to apologize to your Scottish granny."

"I think she'd understand." Libbie's fingers worked at her tousled hair. She could blame its disorder on the wind blasts from the jet.

Cole's hand reached out and stilled her fingers. "Then I'm glad it happened. It's what I've wanted ever since I first saw you."

"At the hearing yesterday?"

"No, before that. When you tried to stab me with your umbrella."

Libbie couldn't see Cole's face in the darkness, but she knew he was smiling. "Have a safe trip to Paris," she said. "And don't let anybody grab your briefcase. Or that piece of chocolate cake."

He laughed. "I'll try not to."

He bent and kissed her lips, so quickly it was over almost before she realized he'd done it.

"I'll call you as soon as I get back from France. I have a lot to do this time, so I'll be gone for two or three weeks." His fingers smoothed the silky curls at the nape of her neck. "I can't call you while I'm gone. Every move I make on this trip will be classified."

"That's okay." Libbie wondered if he'd call even when he got back to Washington. Yes, he'd call. He had to. He couldn't kiss her that way and not feel what she felt. Or could he? Men were unpredictable when it came to things like that. An old memory rose to haunt her, bringing a fresh, painful sense of loss. Would she ever see Cole again, or would he simply disappear from her life the way—? She felt tears spring to her eyes and was grateful for the darkness.

"I've got to go. The pilot is waiting for me." Cole lifted her hand to his lips and pressed a warm kiss into the palm. Why was it so hard for him to say goodbye and leave her? "Libbie?"

"Yes?"

"I'm glad you never went back home to California." Before she could reply, he gave her a hug and turned to go.

While tears spilled down her cheeks, she strained to hear Cole's footsteps loping down the runway.

Chapter Five

The days passed with all the speed of an Alaskan glacier. When it seemed to Libbie that surely a month must've gone by, she got out her calendar to figure out how long it'd been since Cole had left for Paris. To her chagrin, it hadn't yet been a whole week. She tried to lose herself in her work—there was certainly plenty to do, with congressional hearings on the nuclear defense system scheduled for mid-December—but for once, work offered no solace to Libbie.

She knew that Jill was more aware of Libbie's doldrums than she let on. Jill had asked a couple of questions upon Libbie's return from the Panhandle trip with Cole, but when Libbie gave evasive answers, Jill respected her apparent need for privacy and made no further inquiries.

The bleak, dun-colored November days crept forward to the Thanksgiving holidays, then into December, and still Libbie had had no word from Cole. She decided that he must've returned to Washington by now and obviously had no interest in continuing their relationship. Perhaps it was for the best, she thought. She was faced with the biggest challenge of her professional career, tackling things she'd never done before to be sure the Coalition made an effective presentation opposing the nuclear project. She needed to keep her mind on what she was doing instead of daydreaming about a certain military officer whose position was exactly 180 degrees opposite to hers.

Who do you think you're kidding? she derided herself. Work or no, ideology or no, Cole Matthews had gotten under her skin. As a man, he was everything a woman could ever want; as a militarist, he was anathema to Libbie. How was she ever to resolve this agonizing clash between her head and her heart?

She tossed aside her pencil and went to the window of her office. Cars sped past in the heavy noon-hour traffic, but Libbie didn't notice. Her vision was turned inward, to the memory of Cole grinning at her as he waited for her to catch up with him on Dan Williamson's rutted farm road; of Cole taking her muddy shoes and giving them the same military spit polish he gave his own; of Cole laughing down at her as they kick-stepped to the Cotton-Eyed Joe; of Cole with powdered sugar on his lips as he devoured a croissant; of Cole warm and strong against her in the dark hangar....

She buried her face in her hands and let the tears fall. Everybody else had gone to lunch, and she could cry in privacy.

I don't know why, but I feel better, she thought when the tears had spent themselves. She went down the hall to the rest room, splashed cold water on her face and tried to repair the damage with makeup. Her eyes were still a little red, her breath a little shaky, but maybe everyone else would be too preoccupied with their own work to notice.

When the main line of the telephone rang at the receptionist's desk, Libbie wasn't going to answer it. It wasn't one o'clock yet, and the office was officially closed. But it rang so many times that she finally relented and picked up the receiver. "Coalition for Nuclear Sanity," she said. "May I help you?"

"Well, that depends," said a familiar husky baritone. "Just what did you have in mind?"

Libbie's heart stopped for a full beat, and when it started again, it pumped erratically, its rhythm thrown off by her sudden emotional reaction. "Cole!" Maybe she should've tried to play it cool, but she couldn't help herself. Her joy at hearing his voice was too great. "You're back!"

"Just this minute," he said. "I got off the plane and came straight to the Pentagon. I haven't even been to my apartment yet."

"Talk some more," Libbie said. "It's so good to hear your voice again."

"Have you missed me?"

She knew if she could see his face, his characteristic grin would be in place. He sounded as glad to hear her voice as she was to hear his. "Missed you? Not exactly." She didn't intend to sound coy. It was simply that the words "missed you" didn't do justice to her feeling of bereavement.

"Libbie, I haven't slept in thirty-six hours. I just got to town, and I haven't even reported to my commanding officer yet. As far as the Army's concerned,

I'm A.W.O.L. while I'm making this phone call. So don't you dare waste our precious time playing games with me. Tell me the truth. Did you miss me?''

He sounded tired and peevish. And something more, but she couldn't quite put her finger on it. Nervous, maybe—but why? Could it be that he was as anxious about whether her feelings toward him had changed during the past month as she'd been about his? She felt a smile work its way through her body until even her toes curled.

"Of course I missed you," she said, her voice dropping to a purr. "And sometimes I thought maybe I'd imagined the whole thing and I'd never hear from you again."

She heard a soft sigh of relief. "I told you I'd call as soon as I got back. Didn't you believe me?"

"I knew you meant it when you said it. But guys say things like that all the time and never—"

"Dear, sweet Libbie. What kind of guys have you been hanging out with, anyway, that you can't trust a man's promise?" She heard in the background the rustle of papers and another man's voice. "Libbie, I've got to go. I told you I haven't reported for duty yet, and Colonel Jackson is waiting for me. I'll call you later, okay? Probably in the morning."

"I'll be waiting," she said softly.

"Libbie?"

"Yes, Cole?"

"I missed you, too, sweetheart."

When Jill came back from lunch, Libbie was still sitting at her desk, holding the telephone receiver in her hand with a sappy grin on her face.

"Did you just find out you've won the New York lottery?"

"Oklahoma Sweepstakes," Libbie answered, still bemused.

"What are you talking about?"

"Cole just called. He's back from Paris." Libbie dropped the receiver back into its cradle and hugged herself with sheer joy. "Oh, Jill, I was so afraid I'd never hear from him again."

Jill sank down in the chair across from Libbie's desk and put her fingertips to her temples. "Now, let me see if I have this straight," she said. "Cole—that is to say, Colonel Matthews—has just called you from Washington?"

Libbie nodded. "He's been in Paris ever since the day I came back from that trip to the Panhandle with him."

"Why did he call?"

Libbie smiled, her blue eyes crinkling at the corners. "Why, just to let me know he was home. And to tell me he'd missed me."

"He didn't say anything about the congressional hearings scheduled for next week?"

"He didn't have time. He had to report for duty. He said he'd call me again tomorrow morning." For the first time, Libbie noticed the frown on Jill's face. "What's wrong, Jill?"

"I didn't want to pry, Libbie, so I haven't asked you any questions about that Panhandle trip. But remember, I warned you that Cole Matthews is the Pentagon's number-one lady-killer. Is there any possibility that—well, I don't know how else to say it. Do you think he may have stirred up your feelings so he can use you?"

"Use me? How?" Libbie tried not to remember that the same thought had tortured her own mind more than once during the long month just past.

Jill got up and went to the window. She didn't want to see Libbie's face when she made the statement that was going to cut her to the quick. "I told you Cole tried that trick on me, and I nearly fell for it. He gave me a big come-on, took me out dancing and stole a few kisses in the moonlight. And all the time he was trying to get information from me about the Coalition's plans." Jill leaned her head against the window frame and stared out the window. "I thought he was interested in me, but he was only a spy."

When Jill turned toward her, Libbie was shaking her head. "No, Jill, you're wrong. I haven't told him anything about our work, and he didn't ask. You're being unfair."

Jill realized it was pointless to argue. "I hope you're right, Libbie. I hope he's changed. But be careful, won't you? I don't want to hurt your feelings, but our work is too important to be destroyed by a Trojan horse. I had to warn you."

Libbie felt sick at heart. "Of course you did. I understand." She glanced down at the stack of papers on her desk. They'd been sent to her by the Pentagon the first week of Cole's absence, obviously at his direction. The papers were a compilation of all the research data that formed the basis for the environmental impact statement. Libbie remembered how pleased she'd been when the papers arrived. Many of the documents were items the Coalition had tried to obtain through the Freedom of Information Act, but the process was so time-consuming that they hadn't yet been able to get access to all the data. Libbie had supposed it was thoughtfulness on Cole's part to save the Coalition the time and expense of obtaining the materials themselves. Had the gift been a Trojan horse instead? And had that trip to the Panhandle been another? She felt hopelessly confused. She needed to get out of there so she could think.

"I haven't been to lunch yet," she said to Jill's retreating back. "I think I'll go get a bite to eat."

Jill turned and gave her a sympathetic glance. "Sure," she said. "You've been working a lot of overtime lately. Why don't you take the rest of the afternoon off and have yourself a long run through the park or go out to the mall and do some Christmas shopping."

Libbie looked with dismay at the work on her desk. "I have too much to do, Jill."

"Nothing that won't wait until tomorrow." Jill walked back across the office and put an arm around Libbie's shoulder. "It's okay, Libbie. Maybe I'm wrong. It wouldn't be the first time."

"Well, just in case you're right, I'll be careful of what I say." Libbie lifted her head and tried gamely to smile. "But Jill, I have to keep an open mind and give him a chance. I owe him that much. Besides, I hope you're wrong. It's pretty flattering to think the most gorgeous man on four continents can't wait to telephone because he's missed me so much."

There was a strategy session in the conference room the following morning. Libbie and Jill were present, as were representatives from other antinuclear organizations in Central Texas. The upcoming congressional hearings in Washington required a united effort and a pooling of resources, both of which were proving difficult to attain. As with any political effort, there were almost as many ideas on how to achieve goals as there were workers committed to the cause. Factions and splinter groups were a common problem, and today Jill had the burden of trying to achieve consensus and unanimity, at least until the congressional hearings were completed.

Libbie watched her supervisor and friend and felt a growing respect for her ability. Jill seemed to have inexhaustible patience as she labored to smooth out differences and mold a team effort.

"How many of you will be able to attend the hearings in Washington?" Jill asked, aware that financing such trips was always a problem. When only two hands were raised, Jill said, "That will be three of us, then. The Coalition can scrape up the money for my expenses, thanks to a donation from Molly Barnett, the woman whose son was killed in an explosion at a nuclear weapons plant." Jill turned to Libbie and shrugged. "Sorry, Libbie, but the Coalition is almost broke. Only one of us will be able to go."

The news came as no surprise to Libbie. Jill had been working on the books all last week, hoping there was an error in the Coalition's bank balance. The financial picture was grim, and unless more donations came in soon, the office might have to close its doors.

"It doesn't matter," Libbie responded. "I don't know the ropes in Washington, and if only one person can go, it should be you. You're the one who knows all the congressmen and their staffs. My job was to prepare the materials for your presentation." Libbie handed Jill a thick red folder tied with string. "I think you'll find everything you need in here." Libbie didn't mention that at least half the materials had been contained in the bundle sent by the Penta-

gon at Cole's direction. She'd gone through everything carefully last night, and it was all original
research data. Nothing had been tampered with to bias
the raw data in favor of the military. As far as Libbie
could tell, Cole had played straight with her.

"We've heard what a good job you've done on this
project," said Monsignor Kelley, an activist who gave
praise only when it was well deserved.

"She certainly has," Jill agreed. "I don't know
what I'd have done without her."

"Too bad you can't make the trip to Washington,
Libbie," the monsignor said, mulling over the situation. "I wonder if I might be able to find a contribu-
tor or two. . . ."

There was a knock at the conference room door,
and the Coalition's secretary stepped inside. "Excuse
me," she said, "but there's a long-distance call for
Libbie. The operator says it's urgent."

Libbie felt her cheeks flame as everyone turned to
look at her. "I'll be right there, Karen. Transfer the
call to my desk, will you?" She stood to leave. "Please
excuse me," she said to the group of organizers, and
hurried from the conference room.

"Libbie?" said Cole when she picked up the receiver. "Your secretary said you were in a conference."

"I am," she replied. "Why did you say the call was
urgent?"

"So she'd go get you. She didn't want to disturb
you."

Libbie didn't know whether to be angry or amused.
"You know, Cole, you lose some of your charm when
you're so high-handed," she scolded.

"Oh, well, as long as I don't lose all of it. Besides, you know you'd rather talk to me than a bunch of dreary intellectuals and political activists."

She smiled. How did he know the monsignor was such a deadly bore? "These are my colleagues," she said. "And I find them quite stimulating. Besides, we have a common goal."

Cole snorted. "If you've seen one activist, you've seen them all. B-O-R-I-N-G. All they do is quote dead philosophers. Am I right?"

Libbie refused to betray her colleagues, even if his assessment was more or less on target. "Thanks for sending me that packet of research data," she said. "It was a big help. With any luck, you'll be dodging your own bullets for a change."

"At the congressional hearings next week, you mean?"

"Yes, I put together quite an analysis for Jill to present to the House subcommittee."

"Aren't you going to present it yourself?" He sounded annoyed.

"Not this time. The Coalition can't afford to send both of us, so Jill is going alone."

"Damn it, Libbie, you're the one who did the work. Why doesn't she let you go?"

"I don't know my way around Washington. Someone with experience has to go."

Libbie could hear Cole drumming his fingers against the receiver. "There's got to be a way for you to come to Washington," he said. "Let me see what I can work out. I'm sure I can get you on a military flight out of Bergstrom, and maybe the Army can work out some kind of housing arrangement." He sighed. "I wish you could stay with me, but it wouldn't work. We're both going to be in a goldfish bowl, with everybody watching us. I'll figure out something, though."

Libbie was puzzled. Of course she'd like the opportunity to go to Washington, but why was Cole making such a big deal out of it? Was Jill right? Did Cole want her there so he could get information from her? He'd already learned that Jill was a lost cause, whereas Libbie was only too vulnerable to his charms. "Why do both of us need to come?" she asked.

"Because Jill has a one-track mind and hears only what she wants to hear. I think if you come to the Capitol yourself and hear all the different points of view, you'll have a more accurate picture of the problem. Then maybe, just maybe, you'll be able to give better advice to the Coalition when you get back."

"You mean it's a rather elegant form of arm twisting. Is that it?" Libbie asked wryly.

Cole retorted sharply, "You're beginning to sound as cynical as Jill Wagner. What's gotten into you, anyway? I thought you were more open-minded than the ordinary activist."

Libbie was offended by Cole's less-than-subtle putdown of her cause and her chosen career. She fought the urge to make a scathing remark about his regulation-GI military mentality and instead parroted his own words back to him. "If you've seen one activist, you've seen them all." She heard footsteps behind her and turned to see Jill standing in the doorway. Holding her hand over the receiver, Libbie whispered, "Cole says the Army can send me to Washington for the hearings. I guess they think they can brainwash me."

Jill nodded. "Tell him you'll go. I can use your help with the congressional hearings." She waited until Libbie told Cole she'd make the trip to Washington if he could arrange for her travel expenses. Later, when Libbie was off the telephone, Jill said, "Maybe this time *you'll* be the Trojan horse. Won't it be fun if we get to manipulate Cole Matthews the way he's tried to manipulate us?"

Chapter Six

The following Thursday, Libbie put Jill on an early-morning commercial flight to Washington with several of their activist colleagues, then took an afternoon military flight from Bergstrom AFB, arranged by Cole. During a brief telephone call to outline the plans he'd made, Cole explained that the Army had a special budget for important educational projects. The high priority assigned the nuclear defense proposal made Libbie's attendance at the congressional hearings eligible for Army funding.

While Jill and the others would be paying their own expenses at a mediocre Washington hotel, Libbie would be given red-carpet treatment at Concord House, a revamped Victorian mansion in Georgetown operated by a private organization dedicated to traditional American values and a strong military posture. When Libbie did some checking on her own, she learned that Concord House had been established to provide lodging and assistance for visiting dignitaries as a subtle, discreet propaganda tool. She'd have to be very careful, Libbie decided, because it seemed clear she'd been selected for brainwashing.

She stepped off the military plane at Andrews AFB with Jill's last words ringing in her ears: "Keep your ears open and your mouth shut. See if you can't restructure their strategy so that you're the hunter rather than the prey." It was a risky game they were playing, but somehow Libbie knew the rapid thud of her heart had to do less with danger than with the thought of seeing Cole Matthews again.

Libbie craned her neck, hunting Cole in the midst of so many men in uniform, but she didn't find him. Instead she caught sight of a pretty, uniformed redhead holding up a small sign with the words "Libbie Greer?" Libbie stepped out of the flow of foot traffic and made her way to the redhead.

"I'm Libbie Greer," she said, her glance questioning.

"Hi. I'm Amanda Cox. Sergeant Cox, that is." Amanda gave Libbie a ready smile. "Colonel Matthews has been delayed at the Pentagon. I'm to take you to Concord House, and he'll join us there later." Amanda steered Libbie in the right direction, out the exit into a wintry, snow-spangled evening, to a staff car parked at the curb. "Hop in."

A distinguished-looking Army officer spoke to Amanda as they got into the car, and she waved merrily at several other men she recognized. She appeared to be well known and well liked, and Libbie found herself responding to the other woman's warm, vivacious personality. "Are you stationed in Washington?" Libbie asked.

"Oh, yes, and I love it here." Amanda stowed Libbie's suitcase in the trunk, slammed the rear passenger door and scrambled into the driver's seat. "The Pentagon vibrates with power—it's exciting." Amanda pulled the car into the traffic and smiled over her shoulder at Libbie. "When I was nineteen, I thought a man had to be handsome to be sexy. Now I realize that raw power is the real turn-on."

Libbie slid into the shadows of the rear seat to think about Amanda's words. What about Cole, who was both handsome *and* powerful? Amanda must consider him the ultimate turn-on. It was the first time Libbie had given thought to Cole's life apart from his work opposing her on the nuclear defense project. Now she'd stepped into his world, even if only momentarily, and it was totally different from what she'd expected. Here he was not only a man among men but a desirable quarry for attractive women. "Do you work with Colonel Matthews?" she asked.

"Oh, yes, quite frequently," Amanda answered. "We're assigned to the same section. His job is intelligence; mine is entertainment." Amanda slowed for a car turning in front of them, its wheels skidding on the wet pavement. "Back home in Tennessee I'd have honked my horn at anybody who pulled such a dumb stunt," she said. "But not in Washington. You never know whether it might be some crusty VIP who'll get revenge by cutting your budget." Amanda smiled sweetly at the other driver as she pulled into the left lane and passed him. "Good thing I behaved myself," she said. "That was Senator Hubble."

Amanda continued a nonstop commentary on the Washington scene, embellishing items of gossip that she thought might amuse Libbie and at the same time pointing out the famous landmarks.

"What did you mean when you said your job is entertainment?" Libbie asked when she could get a word in edgewise.

"Oh, I'm sort of an unofficial hostess. You know—pick up visiting dignitaries, see that they have a good time, show them the sights." Amanda's eyes caught Libbie's in the rearview mirror. "They usually assign me to visiting males," she said, laughing. "I've been here two years, and you're the first woman I've chauffeured." Amanda made the turn onto Pennsylvania Avenue that would take them to Georgetown. "But Colonel Matthews said he'd take personal charge of your entertainment while you're here." Something in the tone of her voice told Libbie that this visit was being handled differently from their routine procedures.

"I thought you said Cole's job was intelligence," Libbie commented, trying to sound casual. She'd been waiting her chance to pick up on Amanda's earlier throwaway remark.

"Well, so it is. He's always been in intelligence. That was his specialty when he was a Green Beret. But even Colonel Matthews is allowed a little fun now and then. Just be glad you're the lucky lady who gets to share it with him."

Libbie shrugged in feigned indifference. "I suppose he's married."

"He used to be." Amanda chose her words with care. "He's not married anymore, but no one seems to know anything about it. He never talks about his personal life." She made a slow turn around a corner away from the Mall into an area of government buildings. "Now, if you want to know about his Army career, that's easy."

Libbie tried to read Amanda's expression in the glow of a street lamp but found it impossible. "Why is that?" she asked.

Amanda chuckled. "Because a soldier carries his military history around on his uniform for everyone to see."

"He told me he had a Good Conduct Medal." Libbie blushed, remembering Cole's passionate kiss in the hangar and hoping Amanda would never guess the circumstances under which he'd mentioned that particular medal to Libbie.

Amanda's countenance didn't change. "It's like him to be modest," she said. "Didn't he bother to mention his Distinguished Service Cross, his Silver Star, his Bronze Star, and his Distinguished Service Medal?" She paused to consider Cole's many decorations. "Or his RT Anaconda patch? I think he's probably proudest of it."

Libbie hated to admit her ignorance. "Why is that?" she asked.

"It's the one his reconnaissance team wore in Da Nang. They were an elite group working in small teams behind enemy lines. I guess the Pentagon seems like easy duty after what he went through in Vietnam." Amanda stopped the car in front of an imposing stone mansion. "Here we are," she said, hopping out on the driver's side. "Concord House. Victorian antiques, feather beds, Irish linens and lace, and anything else your little ol' heart desires. Just name it."

A doorman came to carry Libbie's bag and usher them into the stately residence. The entry sparkled with light from a crystal chandelier, reflecting on brass doorplates and furnishings, and a thick Oriental rug cushioned their steps across a gleaming parquet floor. They were greeted by a rosy-cheeked woman whose gray hair was fastened into a neat bun at the top of her head, and Amanda made the necessary introductions.

"Libbie, this is Mrs. Miller. She'll take good care of you while you're here."

Mrs. Miller nodded to the doorman, who went ahead with Libbie's bag. "Would you like a cup of tea, dear?" she asked. "I've just brewed a fresh pot." Mrs. Miller's hands moved quickly, with no lost motion, and she poured tea into three elegant, hand-painted cups on a lace-lined silver tray. "Come rest by the fireplace for a minute before you go to your room to freshen up," she said. "Oh, and here's a message for you. Colonel Matthews called a little while ago."

As they followed Mrs. Miller into a tasteful sitting room, Libbie thought she could easily grow accustomed to such pampering. She read Cole's message, then glanced at her watch. He'd be there in a little over an hour. Libbie sat down on a comfortable chair and watched the flames dance in the fireplace while she sipped her tea.

Amanda showed no inclination to leave, and Libbie wondered whether she would remain until Cole's arrival. Or, worse, did Amanda intend to accompany them to dinner? If Libbie couldn't be alone with Cole, how could she learn anything about his plans for the congressional hearing tomorrow? Amanda seemed to blather constantly, but Libbie suspected her entire monologue was carefully calculated to present the information Cole wanted Libbie to have. Beneath Amanda's femme fatale exterior lurked a woman with a shrewd mind, and she was, after all, an Army sergeant assigned to the Pentagon. Amanda's loyalty was to the military and its objectives. Whatever Cole's plan to charm and disarm Libbie and prevent her from achieving the Coalition's goals, Amanda was undoubtedly part of that plan. Now, how do I handle this situation? Libbie asked herself. Divide and conquer? Is that what I learned in eighth-grade Latin?

Libbie stretched and yawned. "Goodness, I'm tired," she said. "I wonder if I have time for a little catnap before dinner."

"Of course, dear," Mrs. Miller answered, quickly rising. "Let me show you to your room. You can freshen up, and I'll wake you when Colonel Matthews gets here."

Libbie placed her teacup on the tray and turned to Amanda. "Thanks so much for picking me up at the airport. I hope I'll see you again before I leave."

There was nothing Amanda could do except make a cheerful departure.

Well, Libbie thought when she was alone in her room, score one for our team. It may not be what the Pentagon had in mind, but I'm going to have Cole Matthews to myself tonight.

Libbie made good use of the next hour and had no time at all for a catnap. She decided to shampoo her hair to get rid of the smell of cigarette smoke absorbed during the flight, and discovered that her room had a gleaming marble bathroom beautifully fitted with antique brass faucets and hardware. After an invigorating shower she reached for one of the thick, velvety towels, surprised to find it toasty warm from its heated rack. There was a mirrored tray equipped with tiny samples of designer cosmetics as well as a hair dryer on its own brass hook. The Bide-a-While Inn has nothing to compare with this, she thought, indulging herself in good-smelling fragrances and lotions while resetting her hair on the heat rollers she'd brought from home.

She turned on a television set tucked inside a cherry wood Queen Anne high boy, and as she flipped the channels, learned that every station was reporting something the president had said or what some senator or congressman had done in Washington that day. It was disconcerting to find that what would be reported in Austin as "national" news was merely "local" in Washington, and that lengthy coverage was given to stories that wouldn't even make the evening news back home. No wonder Washington politicians develop such colossal egos, she thought. Their every move and thought is blown up in living color for all the world to see.

Someone had removed Libbie's clothing from her baggage while she'd been having tea with Mrs. Miller and Amanda, and everything had been given a quick steam pressing, then neatly placed in the closet. Since Libbie was going to be in Washington such a short time, she'd packed lightly, with only pants for tonight and a heather-blue houndstooth check wool suit for tomorrow's committee meeting.

Covering her shoulders with a towel, she brushed her chestnut curls until they gleamed in the lamplight. She gave herself a quick dusting with bath powder, then shimmied into her fanciest, silkiest underwear before donning dressy black slacks and a full-sleeved ivory georgette blouse, trimmed at its deep-vee neckline with a lace collar. She tilted the floor-length mirror in its cherry wood frame, then turned to check her reflection from every angle. The blouse clung nicely to her rounded breasts; the trousers skimmed her trim waist and dipped to contour her bottom.

You'll do, she thought, putting on a pearl necklace and earrings before adding a little more mascara and a touch of aquamarine eye shadow. You look like a lady, but a sexy one. If you play your cards right, Colonel Matthews will be eating from your hand before this night is over. She sighed with anticipation, and the seductive smile that came to her lips had nothing to do with the search-and-destroy assignment she'd been given by Jill.

By the time the telephone rang to announce Cole's arrival, Libbie was remembering their last physical contact and their farewell kiss at the air base hangar. When she went into the foyer to meet him, her blue eyes were sparkling.

"You look lovely, dear," said Mrs. Miller, Libbie's ubiquitous hostess. "Doesn't she, Colonel?"

Cole stood a moment without saying anything, then cleared his throat. "She certainly does." He extended his hand. "It's nice to see you again, Ms. Greer."

Libbie gave him a dazzling smile as their hands made a brief, pulsing contact. Gone for the moment was her role as adversary, and she rejoiced in the sheer pleasure of seeing Cole again. Tall and erect, he looked resplendent in his uniform, and she saw that somehow he'd found time to shave. His dark eyes glimmered in the lamplight with the same warm gladness Libbie felt, and his grin warned her that once they were free from their chaperon, he'd crush Libbie's body against his in a true welcome to Washington.

"How was your trip?" he asked, making small talk to cover the awkward rush of emotion.

"Fine, thanks. I loved flying into the city at dusk. It was so beautiful to see all the lights twinkling and the monuments lit up."

"Haven't you ever been to Washington before?" Cole seemed surprised. He'd spent more than half his life traveling throughout the world, and a simple trip to the nation's capital seemed old hat to him.

"No, never. It's breathtaking," Libbie answered, feeling again the awe she'd experienced when she'd seen with her own eyes things that before had been only pictures in books. "The plane came in low, and I could see the Lincoln Memorial and the Washington Monument—"

Cole laughed. "We'll have to make time to get you a firsthand look from ground level, instead of the treetop view." He made a mental note. "I'll mention it to Amanda in the morning. Maybe she can take you on a sightseeing trip before you have to go back to Austin."

I don't want to go on a sightseeing trip with *Amanda*, Libbie thought, but said nothing. Mrs. Miller was standing there taking in every word, and it was best to pretend Cole was a casual acquaintance. "I doubt there'll be time," Libbie replied. "The congressional hearings will take most of the day, and I'm scheduled to leave tomorrow evening."

Mrs. Miller went to get Libbie's coat, double-breasted and made of camel hair. "I don't want to rush you," the hostess said to Cole, "but since you have a taxi waiting, you ought to run along."

Cole took the coat and helped Libbie into it, smoothing it over her shoulders and removing tresses of hair that caught in her back collar. His fingers lingered, and her eyes closed. She felt herself leaning against him and abruptly caught herself. "Thank you," she said, pulling away from the enticing crook of his arm. "Where are we going for dinner?"

"I thought I'd take you over to M Street and show you the Georgetown night life," Cole answered. "Maybe surprise you with something different to eat." He looked down at her feet. "Good, you've got on your boots, so we can walk in the snow. It's crisp and not too cold."

They turned to say good-night to Mrs. Miller.

"Just ring the bell when you come in, dear," Mrs. Miller said to Libbie, seeing them to the door. "I'll be up."

"Drop us at Twenty-eighth and M," Cole said to the taxi driver. "We'll walk from there." Though he sat carefully erect in his own corner, Cole's hand reached across the seat to clasp Libbie's. "I understand you got rid of Amanda," he said softly. "She was supposed to chauffeur us this evening."

"Oh, really?" Libbie tried to pretend surprise but didn't quite manage it. She averted her head so Cole couldn't see her grin.

"Umm. She had to tell Colonel Jackson that she'd been dismissed, and now he wonders what's going on. This seems to be the first time we've been outmaneuvered by a visiting lobbyist." There was admiration in Cole's voice, despite his official posture that Libbie had frustrated the Pentagon's plans.

She airily waved her fingers. "Tell him it was a simple case of misunderstanding. How was I to know

Amanda was supposed to chauffeur us tonight?'' She turned to face Cole. ''Or was she supposed to *spy* on us tonight?''

He coughed to hold back a laugh. ''Not spy,'' he insisted. ''She's in public relations, not intelligence.''

Libbie wanted to question him further, but Cole's expression warned her not to probe. She wasn't going to learn anything else, at least not for the moment. ''Look at the crowd,'' she commented, gazing out the window at people dressed in everything from saris to designer-label suits under their coats. ''Are they all doing their Christmas shopping?''

''A few of them, maybe. Most are here for the nightlife. This is where Washington's real social action takes place.''

The driver pulled to the curb, and Cole helped Libbie from the taxi, then leaned across the seat to pay for their ride. ''Sure you'll be warm enough?'' he asked, taking Libbie's arm and screening her body from the wind with his own. ''Don't you have any gloves?''

''I didn't think to bring them,'' Libbie answered, falling into step beside Cole and peering into shop windows as they passed by. ''The winters are mild in Austin, and I never wear a coat more than three or four times a year.'' Snow crunched under her high-heeled black boots, and she dug her free hand into her coat pocket to warm it. The other hand was linked in Cole's, absorbing heat from his.

Tiny snowflakes began to fall from the cloudy sky, and as they walked along they could hear the sound of a jazz piano coming from a nearby club. ''Do you want to stop for a drink first, or are you hungry now?'' he asked.

Her fingers stroked his palm. "I'm hungry *now*," she said with a sexy purr. "This walk has whetted my appetite."

Cole gripped her fingers, then placed both their hands inside his overcoat pocket. "Behave yourself," he said gruffly. "This is a public street, and laws against indecent exposure are strictly enforced in Georgetown."

"I wasn't thinking about breaking the law," Libbie answered, lifting her face to Cole's while inside his pocket her hand rotated against his thigh. "I was thinking about nourishment for the body."

"You could've fooled me," Cole answered, removing their hands from his pocket and dropping hers as though it scorched him. "You'll have to warm your hand in your own coat," he added.

Libbie shoved her bare hand into her pocket. "There's plenty of room for yours, too," she said, checking for a reaction from Cole.

He jostled her through the crowd and stepped inside a stairwell. "I don't know what it is about you," he said, his voice hoarse. "I learned absolute control a long time ago. Hot cigarettes on my back won't make me yell. I don't even flinch if a bullet sings past my ears. But five minutes with you, and I've forgotten everything else except how much I want to make love to you. You're dangerous, Libbie, because you make me lose control."

"Is that so bad?" she whispered, overcome by his admission of vulnerability.

"Look at me," he said. "My hands are trembling, and my heart is pounding like it did when I was a seventeen-year-old kid facing battle for the first time. I went to Paris on an important assignment, and when

I was supposed to be memorizing my codes at night, I found myself thinking about you. Now here we are together in Georgetown, with a major committee meeting ahead of us, and am I thinking about my strategy for the hearing tomorrow? Hell, no. I'm thinking about how I can get you alone without anybody finding out about it!'' He drew a deep, raspy breath. "Come on, Matthews, get hold of yourself before you blow this assignment and your whole mission right along with it!''

Libbie leaned against the brick stairwell and watched a grim expression settle over Cole's face. She'd done what she set out to do and stirred his sexual desire, but it had backfired on her. She found she couldn't seize the moment and take advantage of his temporary weakness. Jill would surely give her a severe lecture, but Libbie couldn't press Cole for information, not now. Even if her plot failed, she couldn't betray her own sense of personal integrity. Cole was a decent man who just happened to be her adversary. She couldn't bring herself to exploit his raw, genuine feelings. If her cause was truly just, it could be won some other way, with honor. But how am I going to explain that to Jill? Libbie thought with a vague uneasiness.

She took a deep breath and reached for Cole's hand. "Hey, soldier," she said softly, "you look like you could use a drink." She pointed over her shoulder at the bar next door. "They've got a good band and a big crowd. You'll be safe in there."

Cole shuddered with pent-up emotions, then took off his visored hat and raked a hand through his dark hair. "They just happen to have the best Bloody

Marys in town," he said, managing a grin. "Come on. The Army's buying."

After their drinks, they wandered hand in hand back down the street. They said little, comfortable with the silence, enjoying the falling snow and the cosmopolitan crowd. When they became hungry, Cole led the way to his favorite Vietnamese restaurant, where they ordered spring rolls and lemongrass chicken. The atmosphere was casual, the food fabulous, but Libbie found herself curious that Cole would want to eat Vietnamese food after his wartime experiences.

"This restaurant has nothing to do with the war," he said tersely. "There are no reminders for me here of Da Nang and Saigon." Realizing that his voice had become sharp, he reached for Libbie's hand across the candle-lit table. "I spent almost ten years of my life in Vietnam, Libbie. I learned to love the people and their culture—including the food. I think lemongrass chicken is delicious, and sometimes I get hungry for it." His eyes scanned the tiny restaurant. "But when I come in here, it's only for food, not to torment myself about the war. Those memories are locked in here." He touched his forehead, then his heart. "They grow fainter with time, but I suppose they'll never go away. And if I'm honest, I guess I wouldn't want them to."

"But why not?" Libbie was aghast that anyone would want to cling to memories of war.

"Because no matter what you've been told, it wasn't all bad," he answered. "I saw courage and self-sacrifice of a kind I'll never see again in a peacetime world. I saw people face death with dignity, and it was their most shining hour. Why would I want to forget those memories of the bravest and best people I've ever met?'' A curtain dropped over his eyes and masked his feelings. "I can't explain it," he whispered. "You would've had to be there to understand what I'm talking about."

Libbie lowered her eyes to her lap. It was an intensely private moment, and she felt almost like a pagan intruding upon a holy shrine. Somehow she knew that the things Cole was saying to her now were things he'd never said to another living soul. She felt that he'd paid her a great tribute, but she didn't know how to acknowledge it. And so she sat in silence, head down, and tried to stop the tears from raining down her cheeks.

"Hey, it's okay," Cole said, lifting her fingertips to his lips. "I didn't mean to lean on you so hard."

Their eyes met, and Libbie shook her head, afraid to speak, lest she weep in earnest. Finally she managed a tremulous smile. "Can we go?" she asked, pushing aside her plate.

"Sure, if you'd like," Cole answered, signaling for their waiter. "What's the hurry?"

"I want to go outside and find a dark corner and kiss you until the hurt goes away."

"But, Libbie, sweetheart, I told you . . . I don't hurt." They were standing now, and Cole was studying her face anxiously.

"I know you don't. But I hurt for you." Before Cole could grab the check, Libbie was out the door.

He caught up with her before she'd gone half a block, and they tumbled down a half flight of stairs leading to a closed shop. In the semiprivacy of a crowd-thronged street, they fell into each other's arms, their mouths clinging hungrily.

"Oh, Cole," Libbie whispered over and over, her lips seeking his, her hands clutching his lapels while she strained against him, as though she could pour her very self through him and bring him peace and healing.

"Easy, easy," he murmured, "it's okay. I'm here. Please, Libbie, don't cry, sweetheart. Oh, God, Libbie, please don't cry anymore." He found her cheeks and tilted her head, then bent and kissed her slowly, gently, time after time until she quieted in his arms. "Now then," he whispered, "everything is okay, I promise."

She shook her head fiercely against his overcoat. "It'll never be okay," she insisted. "Because you'll never be the same again. That scared seventeen-year-old boy you used to be is gone forever, left behind in the jungles of Vietnam."

"Look at me, Libbie," Cole said, forcing her head upward. "Vietnam changed me, sure, but I don't want to be a scared kid anymore. You can't let yourself care about things that are gone forever."

Her expression was stricken. "But I do care. I can't help it."

Cole pulled her close into the hollow of his arm. "Ah, Libbie, you and that big heart of yours. You care too much, my darling, and you mustn't. It'll break your heart."

"I guess it already has." She lifted her eyes to Cole's without trying to hide the compassion and caring she felt toward him.

He backed away, as though he were terrified by the emotions they'd let loose tonight. "I think I'd better take you back to Concord House," he said in an impassive voice. "Mrs. Miller is waiting up for you. Besides, I've got to report to Colonel Jackson before he goes to bed.''

The change in Cole was too sudden and threw Libbie off balance.

''Report? About the evening you've spent with me?'' She felt violated to realize that the intimacy they'd shared would now become the subject of an official military field report. ''Why does Colonel Jackson care about *me*?''

Cole tried to cover his tracks. ''I report to him every evening. It's standard operating procedure.'' He ground out the words, as though the energy behind them would make them true. ''It has nothing to do with you.''

Libbie didn't believe him. All at once the pieces fell into place. She'd been invited to Washington as the Pentagon's guest because she was the inexperienced member of the lobbying team and the one most susceptible to persuasion. They didn't even know her, yet they'd written her off as the weakest link in the chain. Humiliation rose in Libbie like a sulfurous cloud, stinging and suffocating her. It was worse than she'd imagined. Not only did they downgrade her *ability*; they doubted her *commitment*—the very thing that gave purpose to her life.

She felt her body stiffen in outrage. Cole had spent the whole evening wearing down her defenses and trying to gain her sympathy so she'd be less likely to attack him tomorrow. The whole poignant story about Vietnam was probably a fabrication to get her mind off the congressional hearings and deter her from her mission. Why hadn't she listened to Jill and followed orders? All she had to show for the evening was a shattered ego, an aching heart, and no useful information at all. The whole trip had been a failure. She lifted her hand to her face and wiped away the last of her tears.

"Fine," she said in a mocking voice. "And while you report to Colonel Jackson about your evening with me, I'll be working on my notes for the hearing tomorrow." She rushed up the half flight of stairs and flagged a passing taxi. "Never mind seeing me back to Concord House," she called over her shoulder. "I'll see you at the committee meeting in the morning."

Chapter Seven

During the midmorning break, Libbie huddled with Jill and the rest of their group in the hallway outside the House subcommittee hearing room. They rehashed the speeches that had already been made and tried to shore up the chinks in their presentation so the second half would go better.

The first speakers had been professors and theologians opposed to the spread of nuclear weapons in general and the current military project in particular. They had set out an ethical and philosophical basis for opposing the Pentagon on this issue, but unfortunately their remarks had been so theoretical as to set the congressmen to dozing. Because Libbie was the member of the team who seemed to stir the most emotion in an audience, the Coalition decided to shuffle the order of things and put her up at bat next.

Libbie felt a familiar surge of adrenaline and hoped it would give her the edge she needed to rise to the challenge before her. She was determined to prove Cole and his Pentagon superiors wrong about her ability. Maybe she didn't have Cole's experience, but she was just as willing as he was to fight to the bitter end for what she believed.

Having resolved the programming change, Jill beckoned Libbie to a cubbyhole away from the others. "You haven't said a word about last night," Jill said. "I thought surely you'd call and give me a report when you got in."

Libbie squared her chin. "There really wasn't anything to tell, unless you want to hear about soft feather beds to sleep on and brioches and Smithfield ham for breakfast."

Jill's eyebrows lifted. "You and Cole must've had quite a night."

Libbie's laughter tinkled despite her inner fears about her upcoming speech. "I wasn't talking about Cole, silly. I was talking about Concord House. I've never seen such luxury! It's enough to turn a person's head."

There was a knowing look on Jill's face. "That's exactly what it's supposed to do. Coddle you, gratify every whim, put you under a feeling of obligation, and all at once you've lost your fighting edge and they've won the battle."

"It all sounds so...so..." Libbie was at a loss for words.

"Calculating?" supplied Jill.

"Yes. And cynical. Do people really sell out their beliefs in exchange for heated towels and fresh strawberries in December?"

Jill lifted a hand and indicated the crowd of people milling in the hallway. "Look around you. How many of the people who come to Washington were once idealistic and wanted to build a better world? But they got soft and lazy, and their dreams just fell by the wayside."

Libbie shook her head. "It seems so sad. And such a waste."

"Yeah." Jill leaned against the plaster wall, her brow furrowed in thought. "That's why we're different from the fat-cat lobbyists the Pentagon is used to dealing with. We aren't here to grab a hefty defense contract and make ourselves a fast buck. We're activists, underpaid and understaffed. We're used to making do and doing without. We're lean and mean, and they don't know what to do with us."

Libbie's face brightened from an inner illumination. "What you're saying is that we're like the Green Berets!"

"God forbid," snorted Jill. "What on earth are you talking about?"

"I mean, they went behind the lines, cut off from regular supply channels, and tried to win the hearts and minds of the people. Isn't that what we're doing?"

Jill was thoughtful. "In a way, I suppose you're right," she said. "But don't ever repeat that thought to anyone—especially not anybody connected with the Coalition! I don't think they'd be flattered to be compared to a Green Beret."

They laughed. "It's our little secret," Libbie agreed.

"And now for the juicy part," Jill said. "What about Cole? You haven't so much as mentioned his name, and you didn't even look up when he walked into the hearing room this morning. What's going on, anyway?''

Libbie's slim fingers reached to massage her temple. "Disillusionment, I guess you'd call it," she said softly. "I thought he was attracted to me, but it seems I'm just another assignment to him. I've been picked as the weakest link in the Coalition's chain, and his job is to snap me apart so the chain will be useless."

"I'm sorry, Libbie. I hoped I was wrong about him." Jill put a comforting arm across Libbie's shoulders.

"So did I." She uttered a shaky sigh. "I wish I'd listened to you in the first place. I guess he used the same technique on me that he used on you. Dancing and moonlight kisses. It worked like a charm."

A buzzer sounded and people headed back into the conference room.

"Don't be too hard on yourself," Jill said, falling into step beside Libbie. "We all have times when we're vulnerable. It hurts, but you'll get over it."

Libbie clenched her fists. "You know the part that hurts the most? Not that I succumbed to his charms, because I think almost any other woman would've done the same thing. What really hurts is that he thinks my work with the Coalition is some kind of lark. Somehow I'm going to prove to him that my commitment is real and that I'm not the shallow bubblehead he thinks I am."

Jill took note of the sparks of anger flashing from Libbie's eyes. It had been unintentional on Jill's part, but their discussion had given Libbie just the fire she needed. Her forthcoming presentation was going to be dynamite.

* * *

Libbie pulled out all the stops, and more than one congressman found himself squirming in his seat when she talked about his responsibility to the people who'd elected him, the common folks back home. She poured out her heart as she related the death of Molly Barnett's son by an exploding bomb and the fears of Dan Williamson that his crops would be poisoned by radiation. Libbie went through the abysmal safety record of many nuclear plants already in operation, threw in an obligatory reference to Three Mile Island, and hammered away at the Chernobyl nuclear disaster in Russia. Rather than present the issue in terms of right and wrong, as the eminent professors before her had done, she tackled it from a practical perspective. Time after time she pounded away at the safety problems inherent in the Pentagon's nuclear defense project.

"The time to think about safety is *now*," she insisted, "not after there's another nuclear disaster. Gentlemen, Molly Barnett and Dan Williamson don't serve on this subcommittee. They don't have a vote. The only ones who can safeguard the future of this country are the people who *do*—gentlemen, that's you. Please don't take this responsibility lightly." Her voice fell to a whisper, and many a person in the room had difficulty swallowing past the lump in his throat.

"Gentlemen, I close with the words said by one of your colleagues in 1963 when the nuclear test ban treaty was being considered. Do you remember that impassioned speech by the great Senator Everett Dirksen, who'd come to change his mind over the course of the debates? He said, 'I should not like to have it written on my tombstone: 'He knew what happened at Hiroshima, but he didn't take a first step.' Gentlemen, I beg of you, don't let it be said about you that you knew what happened at Three Mile Island, at Chernobyl, and at Hiroshima and did nothing. Please vote against this proposal. Thank you."

The room was totally silent as Libbie made her way back to her seat. The chairman cleared his throat, hurried to the podium and spoke into the microphone. "Our thanks to the gentle lady from Texas for her remarks. This hearing will be in recess until Wednesday of next week." He banged the gavel for emphasis. "Adjourned."

The adjournment was unexpected and created a ripple of whispered comments, but the chairman had slipped out a side door before anyone could question him.

Libbie was still so wound up emotionally that it took a moment for the change in plans to register. "Why did they recess?" she asked Jill. "I thought the Pentagon was supposed to present its side this afternoon."

"Apparently someone at the Pentagon told the chairman they want a cooling-off period before they have to take the stage. I don't blame them, either. You're a tough act to follow."

Libbie smiled with relief. "Did I do okay?" she asked, her insecurity still in need of reassurance.

"If you have any doubt, just look at that grim face headed your way," Jill replied, gesturing at Cole Matthews, who was moving rapidly in their direction.

Before Libbie could steel herself, Cole was at her side.

"I don't know why this country refuses to draft females," he said, offering his hand in congratulations.

"You're one hell of a fighter. The Army could use a few good soldiers like you."

"I think we picked up a few votes today, don't you?" Jill asked, unable to keep the supercilious tone from her voice.

He shrugged. "I wouldn't be surprised." He gave his characteristic smile. "You had six boring lectures to put everyone to sleep and one fiery sermon to wake them up again."

Jill chuckled. "I think we all agree on the day's best performance. You aren't going to be eligible to compete as an amateur anymore, Libbie. You've joined the ranks of the professionals."

"I think she's surpassed most of the professionals," Cole said quietly. "If there was a dry eye in the room when she finished, I sure didn't see it. Come on, I'll buy your lunch and toast your victory."

Libbie gave Jill a stricken look. "Oh, I can't," she said. "We've already made plans."

Cole narrowed his eyes. "Dinner, then."

"Well, no," Libbie insisted, scrambling for an excuse. "Since the hearing has recessed, we can go on back to Austin. Jill has to check out of her hotel before one p.m. so she won't get charged for another day."

"You're going back this afternoon?" Cole said to Jill, who nodded. "There's no reason Libbie couldn't stay another day, is there? She's still got her room at Concord House, and she said she wanted to do some sightseeing."

Libbie wished he wouldn't talk about her as though she weren't there. Why was he asking Jill, instead of asking Libbie herself? She sneaked a glance at him and discovered that he seemed uneasy. Why, he was afraid if he asked Libbie, she'd say no! And he was right. Libbie tried to signal to Jill by shaking her head, but Jill paid no attention.

"Libbie deserves a little fun after all her hard work," Jill responded. "Besides, it isn't going to cost the Coalition any money. Why not?"

"Jill," Libbie grumbled under her breath, "don't do this to me."

Jill turned so her body blocked their conversation from Cole's hearing and whispered, "Libbie, you have to take advantage of every opportunity that comes along. The Coalition can't afford for me to stay in Washington until the hearings resume next week. Stay an extra day and see if you can't worm some information out of Cole, okay?"

Libbie's head rotated from side to side. "Didn't you hear me when I told you what happened last night? I'm no match for him when he turns on the charm. If anybody's going to stay, then *you* do it."

Jill's lips formed a twisted smile. "*I* wasn't invited," she said. "*You're* the one he wants." She turned to face Cole. "Libbie's agreed to stay," she said, ignoring Libbie's hiss of disapproval.

"Great," Cole answered. "Amanda will drop you at the airport this afternoon and then take Libbie back to Concord House. By that time, I'll have made plans for the evening." Cole smiled at Jill and walked away without looking at Libbie. He obviously didn't intend to give her a chance to say no.

Amanda was in a cheerful mood on the drive to National Airport with her female passengers. After depositing Jill for her return flight to Austin, Amanda eased her Army staff car through the heavy traffic and got Libbie back to the foyer of Concord House just in time for Cole's telephone call.

"How was the traffic?" he asked Libbie.

"Terrible," Libbie admitted. "I wouldn't trade places with Amanda for anything. But somehow she got us through it."

"Well, that's Friday-afternoon traffic in Washington," Cole said. "Tell Amanda she doesn't have to chauffeur us tonight. Colonel Jackson has assigned Sergeant Wingate to drive us, and Amanda gets to ride as a passenger. That should make her happy."

Libbie repeated Cole's words to Amanda and saw a pleased smile spread over the other woman's face. Amanda stepped to Libbie's side and spoke into the receiver. "Thanks, Colonel. I owe you one."

He laughed. "No, I owed *you* one. This is in repayment."

Libbie didn't understand what was going on and was even more puzzled by Amanda's next words to Cole. "Tell Sergeant Wingate to wear his dress uniform so we can dance."

"Libbie, are you there?" Cole asked. "Amanda has rounded up a fancy dress for you to wear tonight. I'll pick you up at eight o'clock for the big formal ball at the Pentagon." The line went dead.

Libbie slammed the receiver on its hook. "Doesn't he ever *ask*?" she muttered. "Does he always have to order people around?"

Amanda smiled. "He's been in a position of authority for a long time. I guess he forgets that everybody else isn't in the Army, too." She tried to soothe Libbie's ruffled feathers. "You wouldn't want to miss the Christmas party tonight," she said. "It's for all the top brass and VIP's from Capitol Hill. Come on, let's go see if the dress I brought for you fits.''

Libbie decided Amanda deserved top marks for resourcefulness. She'd had less than two hours between the time Cole had told her what he wanted and the time she picked up Libbie and Jill for the trip to National Airport. Yet in that time Amanda had come up with a ball gown, the necessary undergarments, jewelry, and a pair of shoes. Libbie smiled at her in disbelief. "How did you do all this?" she asked.

Amanda shrugged. "It would've been easy if he hadn't insisted on a blue dress," she said. "We're about the same size, and I could've brought you one of my dresses." Amanda took the swishy taffeta dress from its hanger and held it in front of Libbie. "He was right, though. It's the perfect color for your eyes."

Libbie turned to the floor-length mirror. She dared not ask where Amanda had borrowed the dress. Probably some officer's wife, she mused. It was obviously a designer dress, fabulously expensive, cut from watered taffeta the color of a deep, aquamarine-blue pool. It was not a pale, girlish pastel but rather a vibrant, sophisticated hue that matched Libbie's eyes, brightened her creamy complexion, and made her lashes seem even fuller and darker. "It's gorgeous," she breathed.

"Try it on," Amanda urged. "The general's wife is pretty skinny. I hope it won't be too tight for you."

Libbie stripped off the wool suit and cowl-necked sweater she'd worn to the hearing that morning. With Amanda's help, she wiggled into the tight-busted, strapless formal dress and looked down at her exposed cleavage. "What do you think, Amanda?" she asked. "Am I okay, or am I going to get arrested for indecent exposure?"

Amanda chuckled and shook her head. "It's devastating, all right, but I don't think you have to worry about anything worse than getting pawed by some inebriated politician. I'd be delighted if *I* filled out that dress the way you do!"

Libbie studied her reflection in the mirror from every angle and made a few adjustments to the bodice. If she stood very straight and breathed slowly, the dress was modest enough. It was only when she leaned forward or took a deep breath that she might invite too much attention. She gave Amanda the grin of a mischievous child. "If I can just remember to breathe *out* instead of breathe *in*, I think the dress will do. But if I get mixed up..."

Amanda giggled. "You'll have heads turning either way," she said. She handed Libbie a pair of gold evening sandals. "Size seven and a half. Is that right?"

The sandals fit perfectly. Libbie tried on the entire outfit, gold jewelry and all, sashaying in front of the mirror like a teenager the night before her first prom, while Amanda watched in approval.

"I think I'm going to get a promotion over the Greer assignment," Amanda said, smiling. "You're really going to knock them dead." She glanced at her watch. "Well, let me help you with that zipper, and I'll be on my way," she said. "I've got to go home and find a dress that'll pop their eyes out. I can't let you have the limelight all to yourself." She helped Libbie out of the dress and was on her way to the door when she stopped. "I just remembered," she said, reaching inside her pocket. "Here's a note from Colonel Matthews. He said to be sure to give it to you before you get dressed for the ball." Amanda was too well trained to wait to see what the note said. The door closed behind her.

Libbie replaced the ball gown on its hanger, then opened the note. She'd never seen Cole's handwriting before. The heavy black letters were forceful, angular, precise. "No perfume," she read. "I brought some back from Paris for you." The note was signed "Cole," with the signature underlined. When Libbie went into her bathroom to fill the tub, her mind was confused and her heart was racing.

About seven-thirty, Mrs. Miller tried to get Libbie to eat a bite of supper, but Libbie declined. She was afraid if she put one morsel of food in her mouth, she'd never be able to zip her dress. Instead of thinking about her hunger, she concentrated on her party makeup, which was more vivid than the daytime makeup she'd always worn when she was with Cole. She added blusher, eyeliner, and lots of dark mascara, then fluffed her shining hair into curls that fell across her back. At five minutes before eight, she slipped her gown over her head and asked Mrs. Miller to help with the zipper in back while Libbie sucked in her stomach. While Mrs. Miller murmured compliments, Libbie adjusted the tulip skirt around her hips, the snug bodice over her bare breasts, then let Mrs. Miller fasten a wide, bracelet-style gold band around her neck.

Smiling as she pirouetted before the mirror, Libbie asked, "Will I do?"

"Oh, my, yes," her hostess replied. "You'll be the belle of the ball."

The doorbell rang, and Mrs. Miller hurried to the foyer. It was precisely eight o'clock.

Libbie's telephone rang. "Colonel Matthews is on his way to your room, dear," said Mrs. Miller. She didn't sound disapproving, though a male visit to the bedroom of a female guest was not protocol at Concord House. Before Libbie could hang up the receiver, she heard Cole's footsteps in the hallway outside. He knocked just as she opened the door, and for a moment they simply gazed at each other's splendor.

For Cole was not to be outdone by Libbie in her finery. He stood tall and square-shouldered, lean and lithe, in his winter dress uniform. Gone was the Army green, replaced by a dark-blue coat and service cap, and light-blue trousers with a gold officer's stripe down the leg. Instead of his tan poplin shirt, he wore a starched white one with a black four-in-hand tie. There were more medals and battle ribbons on his chest than Libbie could count. As always, his black shoes had a spit shine. He was incredibly handsome, his dark eyes blazing with desire, his lips twisted in a cocky grin.

Libbie's hand lifted to her breast, as though to calm the flutter of her heart. "Hi, soldier."

"Hello, beautiful," he answered, taking her hand from her breast and lifting it to his lips for a welcoming kiss. "Let me look at you." He lifted her hand above her head while she twirled before him, her skirt swishing with each movement. "No wonder Amanda said it wouldn't matter if she went to the party stark naked," he said in a bantering voice. "She said nobody was going to pay attention to her anyway, not with you in the same room."

Color stained Libbie's cheeks. Cole was deft at the art of flirtation, and his compliments pleased her, though they also made her feel shy. "Thank you," she said, not knowing how else to respond.

"For you," he said, taking his free hand from behind his back to offer her two packages, both gift-wrapped in white vellum with gold lamé ribbon. "Open the little one first."

Libbie tore open the wrapping to find a tiny crystal perfume bottle, its gold-plated cap engraved with the logo of a well-known Paris salon. "Oh, Cole, this must be monstrously expensive," she said, removing the lid to breathe in the luxurious scent of lilies-of-the-valley. She lifted the dropper to her earlobe, but Cole reached out to stop her hand.

"I'll do it." His eyes raked her face as he took the dropper from her, touched it to his own finger, then reached out to brush behind one of Libbie's ears, then the other. Without saying a word, he replaced the dropper in the bottle, shook it and once again let the perfume drop onto his finger. This time he slid his hand along her throat line with a lingering caress, moved to the sensitive skin at her temples, then to the inside of her wrists and elbows. By the time he finished, she was trembling with arousal.

"One more pulse point," he said, his voice strained and taut. "Over the heart." He reached out to touch the flesh at the midpoint of her bodice.

Libbie's senses reeled, anticipating his touch, and she lifted her eyes to Cole's. Unconsciously she leaned toward him, drawn by the invisible magnetism that pulsed between them.

His palm opened, as though he would cup her breast and experience its softness. Then his fist clenched and he forced his hand behind his back. "That's enough," he said. "The clerk said when the perfume is so expensive, it only takes a little.'' He managed a mocking grin. ''Now I'm going to have to wash my hands or people will be wondering about my masculinity.''

Libbie was still lost in a mist of enchantment. ''I've always loved the way you smell,'' she said, not realizing that her face was radiant with desire. ''You smell like moss and woods and heather and spring rain— and something else, but I don't know what it is, something very male—''

''Libbie, don't,'' Cole said. How could he tell her that what she smelled was the passion she always roused in him? If he admitted that to her, that same passion, now barely checked, would burst out of control. ''Libbie, I'm going to wash my hands. Go ahead and open your other present.'' He stepped into her bathroom and splashed his face with cold water, then scoured his hands as though he could scrub away the feel of her skin. He didn't go back into the guest room until he heard her rip the paper on her gift.

''Cole, it's beautiful,'' she cried, removing a short evening cape from its tissue-lined box. The cape was made of fragile ivory lace, heavily beaded with gold and silver sequins and pearls, and lined with blue-green velveteen that blended with her dress.

''Do you like it?'' he asked, satisfied with the brilliant smile she gave him in response. ''I walked the streets of Paris trying not to think about you, but everywhere I turned there was a reminder. I saw this in a window, and the lining was exactly the color of your eyes.'' He shrugged. ''So I went in and bought it.''

Libbie's eyes sought his. ''But the perfume—I've never worn anything like this before,'' she said. ''How could it remind you of me?''

"Because it's so fresh and sweet, like the person you are." Cole coughed to hide the emotion that was threatening once again to break loose. "Here, let me help you with the cape. We need to be on our way. Amanda and Tom are waiting for us in the lobby."

Libbie gave Cole a puzzled glance. She never knew how to react to his sudden mood swings, and she didn't understand why another couple was going to the ball with them. Libbie had been left behind in Washington with strict orders to find out the Pentagon's plans regarding the congressional hearings next week, and she'd counted on enough privacy to accomplish her mission. "Who's Tom?" she asked.

"Sergeant Wingate, our chauffeur. He's also Amanda's escort for the evening." Cole wrapped the evening cape around Libbie's shoulders and smoothed it into place, then snapped the pearl-encrusted velveteen fastener.

"He's Amanda's escort, or they're both our *chaperons*?" Libbie asked warily.

"Either way you want to put it." Cole figured he might as well lay all the cards on the table.

"Is that your order from Colonel Jackson?"

Cole shook his head. "No. Those are Amanda's and Tom's orders from *me*."

"But why, Cole?" Libbie felt confusion envelop her like a fog.

His jaw clenched, and he tried to mask the yearning ache he felt. "Because when I'm alone with you, I lose control."

Libbie searched his expression for clues. Even though his words were flattering to her ego, she was suspicious. There was more to this than he was telling her. And then Libbie understood. Cole was smart enough to figure out why Jill had made her stay behind in Washington. He knew Libbie was supposed to act as a spy. By keeping Libbie surrounded with Pentagon people, Cole could keep her from gaining any useful information. At the same time, they could wear her down with their clever battle of attrition, waged with the unconventional weapons of flattery, sensuality, and luxury. When are you ever going to learn? she berated herself. How many times is Cole Matthews going to make a fool out of you before you realize that this is all a big game to him?

Libbie took a deep breath and smiled into Cole's eyes. She might not be as adept at this game as he was, but she was learning fast. "We'd better go before everybody starts wondering what we're doing in here," she said, taking a sidelong look at the four-poster bed. "Besides, the feather mattress is too much of a temptation when you're here with me." She stood on tiptoe and ran her tongue across his lips. "I mustn't kiss you," she said huskily. "I might get lipstick on your collar." Before he could reply, she hurried out to join their chaperons.

So striking a couple were Libbie and Cole that even in a VIP crowd at the Pentagon, every head turned to watch their entry. They made their way down the receiving line, and Libbie found herself capable of imitating Cole's charming blandishments with every person in line. Cole proudly introduced her to generals, admirals, and military attachés, all spectacular in full-dress uniform. He also saw to it that she met the vice-president, the secretary of defense, and the chief of staff. Not bad for a small-town lobbyist, she thought to herself. If only Granny could see me now.

Libbie shook the next hand and offered a smiling compliment to the politician's wife. From beyond her shoulder she heard someone say to Cole, "Why, Colonel Matthews, you old jungle dog, where have you been hiding this Texas beauty? Make her feel at home, why don't you? There's good champagne if you'll ask a waiter."

"How does it feel to be the hit of the evening?" Cole whispered against her hair as he signaled for champagne.

Libbie smiled demurely. "You'll have to ask Amanda if you want the answer to that question." They turned to watch the smashing redhead wander across the room, her hips wiggling provocatively in a backless dress of black silk organza that floated around her shapely, black-stockinged legs.

Cole laughed. "I don't know whether I'm going to end up with a promotion or be relegated to KP," he said. "Nobody's ever shown up at one of these bashes with *two* knockouts before. I'm the envy of every man in the room."

Libbie took the deep breath that made her bodice cling tighter and caused any male watching her to anticipate whether she'd be left daringly exposed. "And I'm the envy of every *woman* in the room," she murmured. "You're more dashing than ten other men combined." She lifted her stemmed glass in a toast. "To you," she whispered, her eyes glittering with an ardor that wasn't entirely feigned.

Cole reached out to brush her lips with his forefinger. "And to the gentle lady from California," he replied, "whose heart is as big as her adopted state of Texas."

Libbie felt tears spring to her lashes. Although she'd been teasing, his endearment was genuine. She averted her head so he wouldn't know she'd been deceitful. Somehow she drank the toast without choking, but it took all her willpower. When the band began to play, she said, "It's a waltz, Cole. Let's dance."

"Don't you want to wait until they play the Cotton-Eyed Joe?" he asked with a grin, then slipped his hand around her waist and led her onto the dance floor. Before they'd gone halfway around the room, someone cut in. "Watch your step," Cole said, relinquishing Libbie. "The general has two left feet." The general was followed by an admiral with good sea legs but no sense of rhythm, then an Egyptian diplomat, a French attaché, and four Washington politicians before the band finished their set and Cole came back to rescue Libbie.

"Having a good time?" he asked.

"Delightful," she responded. It was a heady experience, to receive exaggerated compliments from men whose reputations were publicly acclaimed and whose photographs were often in the newspaper. Yet none of them had the same effect on her that Cole had. One searching glance from him and she felt herself trembling in eager response. There was a magic in the feel of his body against hers, the pressure of his arms around her. When they danced, she wanted the music never to end, the evening never to draw to a close. What you want is an impossible fantasy, she admitted to herself. You want the Army to disappear, the Coalition to go away, the past to be forgotten, the future to be bliss. Open your eyes to the real world, Libbie Greer. Wake up and smell the coffee.

"Coffee?" Cole asked, his expression puzzled.

"Sorry, I was mumbling to myself," Libbie answered. "I was wishing we could dance till morning, with no one to disturb us."

Cole gave her a wicked grin. "It's not very flattering to a guy to think you want to *dance* all night."

"Ah, but you're such a good dancer," she said mischievously.

"I have other talents, too." He pulled her into the shelter of a support column and buried his face in her hair. "Shall I enumerate them?"

"Not unless you can guarantee that everyone will ignore us while you give a hands-on demonstration," she said, her breath coming faster.

Cole tilted her chin. "I don't dare kiss you. You'll get lipstick on my collar," he said, mimicking her earlier statement.

"They have stuff that'll remove lipstick," Libbie countered. She parted her lips, then let her tongue dart out to lick them.

Someone beside them coughed loudly. "Sorry to interrupt, Colonel," said Amanda. "Colonel Jackson asked me to get you."

Cole uttered an oath under his breath and hurried across the room.

Libbie sighed. "You weren't interrupting anything, Amanda. We were just indulging ourselves in a fantasy." She watched Cole make his way to a group of officers whispering urgently in a corner. As soon as Cole joined them, they went to an adjacent small room and shut the door.

Amanda went through the vivacious small talk that was her stock in trade, trying to distract Libbie until further orders were forthcoming. It wasn't long before Cole rejoined them, Sergeant Wingate in tow.

"Sorry, Libbie, but something's come up. Sergeant Wingate will take you back to Concord House when you're ready to go." Cole turned to Amanda. Though there was obviously some emergency, Cole didn't betray it by so much as the flicker of an eyelash. His voice was calm, his manner easy going. "Work out a schedule for tomorrow morning," he said. "Take Libbie on a sight-seeing trip and plan to have lunch. I'll join you as soon as I can." Cole turned to Libbie with an affectionate grin. "Remember where we were," he said. "We'll pick up our conversation at the same point."

Chapter Eight

The following morning, Amanda pulled into the underground parking garage at the Air and Space Museum. It was ten o'clock, opening time for most of the museums and memorials that drew tourists to the nation's capital. Because it was so near Christmas, the crowds were smaller than usual, but already people were beginning to line up. All the buildings looked as though they'd just been sandblasted, so fresh and clean were they, and with light snow sparkling on all the greenery, Libbie thought she'd never seen anything more lovely. In sheer exhilaration she threw out her arms. "It's the most beautiful sight I've ever seen," she exclaimed.

Amanda glanced around at the concrete walls of the parking garage, then turned to Libbie with an amused look.

Libbie's merry laugh rippled and echoed through the ramps and stairwells. "I meant the *city*, not this garage," she said, laughing again. "Most old cities are dirty and run-down. Everything here is so much prettier than I'd expected."

"I'm glad you haven't been disappointed," Amanda answered, smiling as she pointed the way to the elevator that would take them upstairs. "What do you want to see first?"

Libbie pondered. It was a tough decision. There wouldn't be time for much sight-seeing. "I'd like to see the dresses worn by the First Ladies and go to one of the art museums," she said. "And to see Arlington Cemetery and the Lincoln Memorial. Do we have time for all that?"

"I think so. The museums are all nearby, so we'll start with them. Then we can take the Tourmobile over to Arlington and finish up at the Lincoln Memorial." They stepped off the elevator. "Sure you don't want to go through the Air and Space Museum?" Amanda seemed surprised that Libbie hadn't mentioned the building where they'd parked the car.

"Is that what everybody else wants to see?" Libbie asked.

"Always. It's the most popular stop."

Libbie was torn. There was so much to see and so little time to do it.

Amanda tried to help. "You probably noticed Lindbergh's *Spirit of St. Louis* suspended from the ceiling when we drove past. You might as well see it up close, since it's right here on the ground floor."

They enjoyed the Lindbergh exhibit, as well as the Wright brothers' *Kitty Hawk Flyer* and the *Skylab* model, then resolutely exited the museum and walked across the Mall. Libbie soon realized there wouldn't be time enough for more than a first peek that would whet her appetite for a second, more leisurely visit to Washington.

"Where do they keep the French Impressionists?" Libbie asked, hunting for a directory as they entered the Rotunda of the National Gallery of Art. A helpful guide pointed them on their way to the special collection of paintings by Monet, Renoir, Degas, and other major Impressionists. Libbie stood transfixed, gazing at original works that had previously been known to her only through inferior prints. "Look at the brush strokes," she murmured in admiration. She stepped back to appreciate a particularly beautiful Renoir from a distance. "From back here," she said, "the separate strokes of blue and yellow look like a single stroke of green."

"Do you paint?" Amanda asked, curious that Libbie seemed so fascinated with technique.

"Oh, no, I have no talent at all. I don't even know much about art. But something in me has always responded to Impressionist painting." Libbie walked a few steps down the corridor to view another painting, this one a river scene with sunlight shimmering on blue water and the white sails of a boat. "I suppose it's because the paintings are so romantic."

Amanda came to join Libbie, expecting to see a picture of young lovers. Instead there was only a sailboat. "Romantic?" she questioned.

"A romanticized view of life, I should've said." Libbie tried to explain herself. "The realistic paintings by earlier artists are dark and somber. Then the French came along with a new approach to art. Instead of being realistic, their paintings create an impression—not life the way it *is*, but the way it *ought* to be, with everything light and beautiful." She shook her head, dismayed that it was so difficult to communicate what she felt. "Sorry," she said. "I don't mean to bore you."

"You're not," Amanda replied. "It's interesting that your personal taste in art reflects your attitude about life." When Libbie's eyebrows lifted in question, Amanda continued. "That's the way I see you, anyway, as the kind of person who wants life to be better than it is and the world to be more beautiful."

Libbie traced circles on the floor with her foot and didn't look up. "I guess I seem pretty naive and idealistic," she said.

Amanda put her arm around Libbie's shoulders in a casual hug. "You certainly do," she said, "and that's what I like about you. It's refreshing to chauffeur someone who's young and starry-eyed for a change. We get plenty and to spare of the other kind." Amanda looked around. The art museum was huge. "Well," she said, "which exhibit do you want to see next?"

"No more paintings today," Libbie replied, walking toward the Rotunda. "After a dozen or so, it all begins to blur. I'd rather look at a few and really enjoy them."

From the National Gallery of Art, they walked in the crisp winter air to the Smithsonian's National Museum of American History, and the more Libbie saw there, the more she wanted to see. On the lower floor were all kinds of machinery, from atom smashers to Eli Whitney's cotton gin. On the next floor, Libbie found the exhibit she'd wanted to see of mannequins in dresses that had been worn by the nation's

First Ladies. Amanda enjoyed the exhibit as much as Libbie did, and they laughed and visualized themselves in the lovely gowns.

"Do you think any of these First Ladies look any finer than we did last night at the ball?" Libbie asked. "I don't see anyone whose bottom might wiggle the way yours did in that black dress."

Their happy laughter attracted the attention of other tourists, who smiled and wondered what was causing so much pleasure to two attractive females.

"My feet hurt," Libbie said, standing on one foot and massaging the other. "Let's find someplace to sit down for a while."

"There's a snack bar in the basement. Let's grab a sandwich," Amanda said, heading in that direction.

"Too bad Cole's not with us," Libbie replied. "He'd go crazy over that old-fashioned ice-cream parlor we passed earlier." She smiled wistfully, remembering Cole with powdered sugar on his lips as he devoured a croissant. "That man has the worst sweet tooth I've ever seen."

They ordered sandwiches and coffee, and while they waited for their order, Amanda excused herself to make a telephone call. When she returned, she said, "The officer on duty says Colonel Matthews will join us about three o'clock, so we've got almost two hours." Amanda sat down, kicked one shoe loose, and massaged her instep.

Libbie took a bite of her sandwich and tried not to show undue interest in the time of Cole's arrival. "Two hours isn't very long," she said. "Will we have time for everything I asked to see?"

"We can ride the Tourmobile out to Arlington Cemetery, and it'll bring us back to the Lincoln

Memorial. That's the last stop on your list, so I left a message for Colonel Matthews to meet us there," Amanda said, sipping her coffee.

Libbie couldn't hold back a radiant smile. "Good," she said softly. She wondered how much time she'd have with Cole. She still didn't know when she was supposed to fly back to Austin. Maybe they'd get to have dinner together. Maybe—

She lifted her eyes to find Amanda watching every change in her expression. "Libbie," Amanda said, searching for tactful words. "I'll be on duty as your chauffeur for the rest of the day."

Libbie blushed. "Am I that transparent?" she asked.

Amanda nodded.

"Is there some special reason we have to be chaperoned?" Libbie asked, studying the toasted bread of her sandwich.

"Libbie, in case you haven't noticed, Colonel Matthews has a devastating effect on women. Sometimes it's an asset, but it can also backfire." Amanda paused, as though trying to find a way to explain her orders without revealing too much. "The nuclear defense project is a major assignment for everybody connected with it. That's why the Army approved funding for your trip as an educational expense. It would be highly detrimental to the project if anyone seemed to be using undue influence on you while you're here on official business. The safest thing to do was assign you a driver and never leave you and Colonel Matthews alone together."

"You left us alone on Thursday night when we went to Georgetown," Libbie said, remembering how pleased she'd been to have outmaneuvered Amanda that day.

"You didn't give me a whole lot of choice," Amanda said ruefully. "But I reported the situation to Colonel Matthews, and I supposed he'd assign Tom Wingate to drive him instead. I was really surprised that he used a taxi, but I guess it didn't matter, because you were in public the whole time. You were never alone together."

"How do you know?"

"It was in the written report."

Libbie pushed a bit of lettuce to the edge of her plate. "Does Cole have a bad reputation for putting moves on women?"

Amanda uttered a strangled chuckle. "Heavens, no!" She sipped her coffee and laughed again. "I'm sure he gets plenty of offers, though."

Libbie felt baffled. Cole was more sensual than any man she'd every met, and his bold charm with women seemed as natural as breathing. Even Jill had come under his spell. Yet with Libbie, who was obviously susceptible to Cole's magnetism, he'd taken care to arrange a situation where her reputation, and her rash desire, would be protected. Libbie leaned her head back against a column. "Did you ever chauffeur Jill Wagner before?" she asked in a curious voice.

"No, I think Tom drove her a time or two. Why?"

Libbie shook her head. "I just wondered." She smiled across the table at Amanda. "Why do you get that light in your eyes every time you say Tom's name?" she asked.

It was Amanda's turn to blush. "Oh, Tom and I, we're—"

"More than friends?" Libbie inquired.

Amanda nodded. "Funny, isn't it. I've spent two years at the Pentagon surrounded by officers, and here I've fallen in love with a sergeant!"

"You're the woman who insists that raw power is the real turn-on. When you told me that, I thought you'd set your cap for Cole."

"For Colonel Matthews?" Amanda exploded in laughter. "No way."

"Why not?" Libbie asked, offended that Amanda wouldn't consider Cole the most desirable man in Washington. "You said yourself he's got a devastating effect on women."

"Well, sure," Amanda agreed. "But haven't you noticed how he uses all that charm to keep a safe distance between himself and other people? He won't let anybody get close to him. I've worked with him for two years, and I still don't know what kind of movies he likes or what he does with his spare time. I don't even know where he grew up. And he doesn't know anything about me, either. He's never bothered to ask. We make a great working team, but I'm not a real person to him. It's almost as though the feeling part of him is dead, and he doesn't want anybody else in his life. All he wants is his work. His mission. The Army." Amanda took a bite of her sandwich, then made a face when she took a sip of coffee and discovered it had gotten cold.

Libbie wondered if she and Amanda were talking about the same Cole Matthews. How could two observers have such opposite impressions of the same man? Cole had allowed Libbie to see his pain and share his anguish. His attention had seemed to rivet on learning everything he could about Libbie. She sighed. Too bad people couldn't be cataloged in tidy niches the way historical artifacts were exhibited in museums. Yet objects in museums could be classified by era because they belonged to the dead past, not the dynamic present. Cole couldn't be put into a category yet, not by Libbie and not by Amanda, because he was still changing and growing. And so was Libbie.

Amanda pushed aside her tray and stood. "If we're going to get to the Lincoln Memorial by three, we'd better get started," she said.

"We wouldn't want to keep Colonel Matthews waiting," Libbie added, smiling in anticipation.

Their visit to the acres and acres of military graves at Arlington National Cemetery, together with a stop at the Kennedy graves and the Tomb of the Unknown Soldier, created a sense of sadness in Libbie. The sheer number of granite-slabbed graves was an overwhelming reminder of the waste and carnage of war. On the trip back to the Mall by Tourmobile, Libbie fell silent. Amanda sensed that something was troubling Libbie and left her to her introspection.

"Here we are," Amanda said when the Tourmobile stopped at the Lincoln Memorial. "And there's an Army staff car pulling up behind the taxi stand."

Libbie tried to shake off her bleak thoughts and looked at her watch. "Right on time," she said, following Amanda off the bus with the other passengers. She could see Cole emerging from the staff car, Tom Wingate in the driver's seat. "You're in luck, Amanda," Libbie said with a grin. "There's your boyfriend."

Cole saw the women exiting the bus and came to meet them, perfunctorily touching his cap in response to Amanda's salute. "Did you have time to see everything?" he asked, smiling at Libbie.

"Oh, no," she answered. "We hardly got started. You could spend weeks trying to see everything." She lifted her eyes to meet Cole's gaze. He seemed fatigued, as though he'd been working very hard throughout the night. "I'm glad I got to stay over," she said softly. "It meant a lot to see all the things I've only read about in books."

"Have you see the Lincoln Memorial yet?" he asked.

She and Amanda shook their heads. "We were going to finish up with it," Amanda answered.

"I'll see it with you, then," Cole said. "It's always the highlight of everyone's trip." He reached for Libbie's hand and slid it through the crook of his elbow, then turned to Amanda. "Ask Sergeant Wingate if he wants to join us." He paused a moment, then glanced at the crowds around them and at all the people walking up the steps to the monument. "Or if you're tired, you can wait for us. We won't be long."

Amanda, too, glanced at the crowds, as did Libbie. "Amanda said her feet hurt," Libbie said, giving Amanda a chance to remain behind with Sergeant Wingate. The women exchanged knowing smiles. "Stay with Tom if you'd rather," Libbie whispered. "I promise not to seduce Cole behind one of the pillars."

"What was all that whispering about?" Cole asked as they crossed the street after leaving Amanda, who was walking with a feigned limp to Sergeant Wingate's car.

"Girl talk," Libbie answered with a breezy wave of her hand.

"You and Sergeant Cox seem to be getting on very well together," Cole noted.

"I like her. We've had a good time today."

"She's a good soldier," Cole said, starting the long climb up the steps to the top of the monument. "Race you to the top." He let go of Libbie's hand and took the steps several at a time while she scrambled to catch up. They reached the top, winded.

"Beat you," he said, wheezing out the words.

"You cheated," Libbie insisted, laughing and panting from exertion. "You started off before I knew we were in a race." She leaned against one of the marble pillars while she caught her breath. "I think I might've beaten you if I hadn't had to dodge those little kids who got in the way."

"Now who's being a sore loser and making excuses?" Cole asked, stretching out his arm and leaning against the pillar with one hand beside Libbie's face. There was a mischievous gleam in his eye.

Libbie fought the desire to turn her head and brush his hand with a feathery kiss. The shadows of the memorial fell across Cole's face, etching lines of weariness and making him seem vulnerable. "You look tired," she said, not responding to his banter.

"I am, a little," he admitted. "But not too tired for another race. Want to see who's first going back down?"

She shook her head. "I concede."

Cole tilted her chin. "Hey, it's not like you to let me off the hook so easily," he said. "What's happened to your fighting spirit?"

"Even fighters get a day off, don't they?" Libbie smiled at him. She was beginning to understand what Amanda had meant earlier when she'd said Cole used his charm as a distancing technique. He wanted to tease and joke now, and somehow Libbie knew he was about to leave her. This was his way to avoid saying goodbye. "Come on," she said, taking his elbow again, "we rushed all the way to the top. Let's at least look at the Lincoln statue while we're here."

They walked over to the marble statue, nineteen feet high, where a thoughtful, weary, and ever-so-human figure of Lincoln sat gazing into the distance. Carved on the walls of the memorial were the Gettysburg and the Second Inaugural addresses. Libbie read aloud the dedication written above the statue. "In this temple, as in the hearts of the people for whom he saved the Union, the memory of Abraham Lincoln is enshrined forever."

"For us, Libbie," Cole said quietly. "Lincoln saved the Union for us. And we have to save it for the people who come after us."

She nodded. "But don't forget what he said in the Gettysburg Address. The Union is supposed to be a government of the people, by the people, and for the people. It has to represent everybody."

They took each other's measure and found they were an equal match. At this moment, neither could win; neither would lose.

Cole reached out to touch a silky strand of hair and push it back from Libbie's cheek. "You smell nice," he said, drawing her a step closer.

"Thank you," she answered. "It's my French perfume."

He cleared his throat. "Not altogether."

Libbie reached for his hand and pressed it to her cheek. "Cole—"

He closed his eyes as though pain had flashed through him. "Don't, Libbie," he said, removing his hand and jabbing it in his pants pocket. "I've been given a new assignment. I have to leave pretty soon. We've arranged for you to take a flight back to Austin tonight."

"Will you be able to ride to the airport with me?" she asked. She'd known this was coming. Why did she feel so empty, so bereft?

Cole shook his head. "I'll be gone before you've packed your bags," he said. "Sergeant Wingate will take me to Andrews when I leave here." Cole turned to look out across the Mall at the Reflecting Pool and the Washington Monument. He kept his head averted and both hands in his pockets. "Jill is going to expect you to come back with some useful information," he said. "Tell her that the Pentagon has requested a recess of the congressional hearings long enough to do an additional safety study. It's going to take about two months, and the information will be presented at a public hearing in Austin before we come back to Congress with it."

A wave of guilt washed over Libbie. Conscience-stricken, she reached for Cole's arm. "Why are you telling me this?" she asked.

"You can't go back to Austin empty-handed," Cole said, uttering a rueful laugh. "And this information will be made public next week, so it doesn't matter if Jill knows about it a little early. She'll think her plan worked and give you good marks for spying on the Army."

"How did you know I was supposed to be a spy?" Libbie wished the marble floor of the monument would open up and let her drop to the underpinnings in the basement. "Was I really so obvious?"

This time Cole's laugh was good-natured. "I'm afraid so," he agreed. "You're too honest and natural to make a good spy. Every time you remembered why you were here, you'd go into a femme fatale act that a junior high drama student could've done better."

Libbie leaned against the marble pillar and collapsed with laughter. "And I thought I was such a Mata Hari," she said. She laughed again, and even Mr. Lincoln seemed to smile as the merry sound caught in the breeze. They walked away from the monument and started down the steps. "But if you knew," Libbie asked, bemused, "then why did you ask me to stay?"

"That was the Army's idea," Cole answered. "Part of the VIP treatment."

"To mellow me and make me forget why I'd come?" Libbie was embarrassed at having her hand caught in the cookie jar, but Cole was no saint himself. He'd had his own secret agenda for this visit, and she now tartly reminded him of that fact. "You thought I was the most likely candidate for recruiting to your side," she complained. "The weakest link in the chain."

"Hold on a minute," Cole said, gripping Libbie's elbow as they reached the bottom of the steps. "You've got it all wrong. You're not the *weakest* link at the Coalition—you're the *strongest*."

The confusion that Cole so often created in Libbie was back. She shook her head to try to clear it. "But Jill—" she protested.

"Jill's smart. She's a good organizer. Her follow-through is excellent. But she doesn't have what it takes to reach out and touch another person's heart," Cole said. "You do."

It was one of the finest compliments that had ever been paid to Libbie. She was always so unsure of herself and her abilities that it meant a great deal to her. "Why, thank you, Cole," she said, experiencing a rush of gratitude that he could make her feel so good about herself and help her recognize a strength that she hadn't even known was there.

He smiled down at her. "Come on," he said, heading toward a kiosk where snacks were sold. "I'll buy you a cup of coffee." He looked at his watch, then toward the staff car, where their two drivers were waiting. "We've still got a little time."

They sat on a park bench sipping hot coffee, their conversation now casual, about nothing in particular. They were preparing themselves for the farewell that neither of them dared mention. The late-afternoon sun fell across Libbie's head and shoulders, warming her in the chilly December air. She pulled her coat more tightly around herself, then slid into the hollow of Cole's shoulder when he lifted his arm and put it around her.

Small groups of people walked past them, their eyes downcast, their expressions solemn. Libbie noticed a pair of women, one young, the other old, weeping as they passed by. "Why are they crying?" she asked.

Cole took a sip of coffee before he answered. "I guess they've just come from the Vietnam Memorial," he said. He gestured to a nearby area where a black granite slab extended along the snow-covered grass.

Libbie winced with a pain that felt almost physical. "I didn't realize it was right here," she said.

"There are two walls. One points to the Washington Monument, the other to the Lincoln Memorial.

They meet in the center." Cole's voice was devoid of expression, as though he were a tour guide presenting factual information.

So here you are, Libbie thought to herself. Without intending it, you've stumbled onto the memorial for the Americans who lost their lives in the Vietnam War. Her hand crept to her throat. Her heart was pumping furiously, and if it hadn't been for Cole's arm across her shoulders, she would've jumped up from the park bench and run in the opposite direction.

"Do you want to go look at it?" Cole asked.

She shook her head. "No," she whispered in anguish. "No. I can't."

He looked down at her, and his face was as tortured as her own. "Drink your coffee," he said. "It'll warm you."

She clutched the lapel of his topcoat as a wave of despair rocked her. "When your heart is frozen, nothing can warm it," she said. Her eyes filled with tears.

"Did you lose someone in the war?" Cole asked.

Libbie nodded. "My brother," she said. "He was only three years older than I was, and we were always very close. I loved him more than anybody else in the whole world."

"Then the best thing you can do is go over there and find his name on the monument. There's no sense trying to run away from the reality of death."

"Will you go with me?"

"No. I'll wait here for you."

She stayed beside him on the bench. "Then I'm not going," she said. "I can't face it by myself."

Cole took her cheeks in his hands. "Libbie, you're so much stronger than you realize," he said in a choked voice. "That great fighting heart of yours is full of courage. Dealing with your grief at the monument is a private matter. I'd be an intruder."

"Cole, please. I need you."

He wavered, then relented. They tossed their cups into the trash can, then walked to the information booth. "This is my brother's name," she said, writing it out for the clerk on duty. "He was killed in 1975."

The clerk checked the records, then jotted down the location. With trepidation Libbie made her way to the west wall, walking past one black granite panel after another, Cole at her side. The impact of the Vietnam Memorial was even more forceful than she had anticipated, for as they walked, the significance of the names mounted and she realized that it was like the sea of marble tombstones at Arlington. Each name symbolized a human life lost on a battlefield far from home.

She stopped at a panel in the center and hunted until she found her brother's name. Her finger reached out to trace the letters, and though she tried to read his name aloud, no sound would come from her constricted throat.

"Douglas McGregor Greer," read Cole. "A good Scottish name." He opened his arms, and Libbie flung herself against his chest and began to weep. He rocked her in his arms, trying to comfort her, and stroked her hair as she whispered incoherently. "Now, now," he murmured. "Go ahead and cry. Don't keep all that hurt locked up inside you."

"He was only nineteen," she said when her sobs began to lessen. "Now he's dead, and all that's left is his name on a granite slab."

She felt a tightening in Cole's arms around her. "Not all the dead have their names carved on that panel," he whispered brokenly. "My best friend's name isn't there. My wife's name isn't there."

"Your wife died in Vietnam, too?" Libbie asked, surprise overtaking her grief.

"She was Vietnamese." A long sigh racked Cole's body. "I knew Saigon was about to fall," he said. "Everybody knew it. I sent Nguyet away to a village I thought was safe, with our baby daughter. Phong Ta—my best friend—was the chief of the village, and he said he'd protect them with his life." Cole took Libbie's hand and they walked to a park bench to sit down. "The Viet Cong must've known Phong Ta's village had helped the Americans, so they raided it the day after they took Saigon. They killed Phong Ta and Nguyet and everybody else they could find."

"And your daughter?"

"I've always wondered if Nguyet had a premonition that her village would fall to the Viet Cong. For some reason she decided to hide baby Lai in another village. When the children were evacuated after Saigon fell, someone got our baby to the boats. It took me two years to find her again. She'd been sent to a refugee camp in Holland." Cole took Libbie's hand in his and squeezed it. When their eyes met, she saw that his face was ashen with grief and pain. He shook his head, as though he could clear it from memories that still haunted him.

"I'm sorry, Cole," Libbie murmured, returning the pressure of his hand. "I had no idea...." She felt an uncomfortable sense of shame. She'd been so quick to judge Cole for being a staunch militarist. Why hadn't she understood that the commitment he brought to his work grew out of motives at least as strong as her own? To suffer the death of his wife and then spend two years searching the world for his lost daughter were tragedies that would change a person forever. "Did your baby daughter remember you when you finally found her again?" she asked softly.

The muscle worked at the ridge of Cole's jaw, and he seemed to be struggling to keep his sorrow in check. "No," he answered in a choked voice. "I was a stranger to her. Still am." He leaned forward and buried his face in his hands. "It hurts too much to talk about it."

Libbie sat quietly, giving him time to pull himself together. Her own pain was overwhelming, and watching Cole's only served to magnify it. They'd both lost too much, and there seemed to be no comfort for these old wounds that had never healed. Instinctively she placed her cheek against Cole's shoulder blade and stroked the rough wool of his uniformed back.

Cole turned and drew her into the shelter of his arm. "What about you, Libbie?" he asked. "What did the war do to you?"

She gripped his hand. "After my brother was killed," Libbie said, "I was angry and bitter. He'd been drafted near the end, when everybody knew we were losing the war. It seemed like such a stupid waste to send a nineteen-year-old boy to die in something that was already over. Did you notice all those names for May 1975? I guess they all died with Doug in Saigon when it fell to the Viet Cong." Libbie bent forward and coiled herself into a ball, rocking back and forth with an inner agony. "I was so carefree until Doug died. Then his death taught me how truly horrible war is. I'll never be the same again," she whispered. "I've vowed to spend the rest of my life working for world peace."

Their fingers intertwined. "And I'm committed to the fight against totalitarianism," Cole answered in a voice as full of resolve as Libbie's. "Even if it takes military force to do it."

It's so ironic, Libbie thought. The same historical event that cost both of us the person we loved most has sent our lives off in two different directions—one to war, the other to peace.

"I respect you too much to try to change your mind," Cole said softly.

Libbie nodded. "Same here."

They stood. "Well—"

"I guess you have a plane to catch." Libbie tried to smile. "Thanks for a lovely time in Washington," she said, offering her hand.

Cole looked at his watch, then lifted his eyes to scan the area. The afternoon was drawing to a close, and people were beginning to depart the Mall. "Come with me," Cole said, drawing Libbie to the shadows of a concession stand that had already closed. He pulled her into his arms. "Two minutes," he whispered. "That's all the time I have left, and I'm going to spend it kissing you goodbye."

Libbie lowered her lashes, trying to hold back the tears. Cole's palms framed her cheeks, and his thumbs stroked the dark hollows underneath her eyes. She felt his warm breath against her hair, and she stepped closer into the circle of his arms, her own arms locked around his waist. Their bodies were encumbered with layers of heavy wool overcoats, but in this moment there was no barrier between their hearts and minds.

"Dearest Libbie," Cole murmured, lowering his head to touch her mouth with lips that were gentle and caressing. "You slipped in when I wasn't looking and stole my heart." He kissed her with a sweet, tender warmth that made her senses purr. She lifted her hands to stroke the bare skin at the base of his neck, then sank her fingers into his thick, dark hair. His scent lured her closer, intoxicating her, and her lips parted underneath his. Their kiss deepened, and she felt Cole shudder in her arms.

His mouth broke away, ending the kiss. "How can I give you up?" he whispered, lifting her against him so that her toes barely touched the pavement. "We have to say goodbye, Libbie," he said in a choked voice. "You have your mission, and I have mine. We don't have room in our lives for each other."

She tried to protest, but his mouth closed upon hers in a fierce, savage kiss that rebuked her dishonesty. "You know this is the way it has to be, don't you?" he demanded. Then he groaned, and she tasted the salt of his tears mixed with her own. His lips brushed hers for the last time, and he loosened his embrace.

When she opened her eyes to look into his, he was struggling to control his emotions. "Cole," she whispered. "Oh, Cole—"

His hand gripped hers so tightly she thought he would crush her bones. "Say it, Libbie," he demanded. "This moment is all we're ever going to have of each other, so tell me. Now."

Libbie thought her heart would surely break when she saw the sorrow in Cole's dark eyes. "Cole, I "

"I love you, Libbie. God knows I didn't mean it to happen, but it did." He tilted her chin and managed a grin. "Our time's run out on us, sweetheart. Are you going to let me leave without telling me you love me, too?"

Her hand worked at her throat, as though somehow she could unleash the words that were stuck there. Cole seized her in a ferocious hug, then set her down and started toward the waiting staff car. Libbie stood, paralyzed, and watched him step into the back seat when Sergeant Wingate opened the car door. Cole turned his head in her direction and gave her a final salute. The car pulled into the lane and made a slow turn. Just as it reached the corner to enter Independence Street, Libbie found her voice. "Cole!" she shouted, running toward the car. "Cole, I love you!" The car continued on its way, and Libbie sank onto a park bench with tears streaming down her cheeks.

She felt a hand touch her shoulder. "Come on, Libbie," Amanda said. "I'll take you back to Concord House to pack your things."

"He didn't hear me," Libbie mourned, weeping into her hands.

"Yes, he did," Amanda said gently. "Didn't you see him smile at you when the car turned the corner?"

Chapter Nine

Libbie heard nothing from Cole for weeks, not even so much as a Christmas card. She went through the holiday season with a heart that was anything but merry, and she found it difficult to attend parties and pretend to be having a good time. Jill tried to get Libbie involved in the season's festivities but gave up when Libbie's excuses became too lame to believe.

There was still plenty of work to do, and Libbie tried to immerse herself in Coalition business. Pleased with Libbie's "success" in Washington, Jill delegated to her some of the preparations for the second public hearing on the nuclear defense project, now scheduled to be held in Austin during February. Libbie lined up speakers and tried to patch some of the tatters among the Coalition membership. As with other organizations, there were always factions and in-fighting to contend with. When Libbie found herself in the role of mediator and conciliator, she gained a new appreciation for Jill's talent in those areas. It was harder than it looked to harmonize conflicting goals and placate overweening egos.

Sometimes Libbie went home at night tired and frustrated over the slow progress being made, and her sleep was often troubled with vague dreams that left her uneasy. The dark hollows under her eyes became permanent fixtures.

"You're working too hard," Jill said one afternoon in early February. "I don't think you're getting enough sleep."

"I'm fine," Libbie protested, pushing her hair back from her face. "I sleep at least eight hours every night. That's more than usual."

"Are you still running every day?"

"Sure. At least two miles." Libbie gathered up a bundle of file folders from the top of Jill's desk and stacked them to go through later in the week. "I like running in the cold winter breeze. It's invigorating."

Jill leaned back in her chair and gave Libbie an appraising look. "You don't look invigorated," she said. "As they say back home in Luling, you look a mite peaked."

Libbie tried unsuccessfully to laugh off Jill's remark.

"You haven't been the same since you came back from Washington," Jill insisted. "Did anything go wrong up there?"

"Jill, please." Libbie didn't want to discuss the trip to Washington with anyone. It was too personal.

"You can't fool me," Jill said. "I kept waiting for you to tell me what had happened, but you've never said a word. You just get more withdrawn with every week that passes." Jill should've sensed that she was treading on fragile feelings, but she didn't. "What happened to you in Washington?" she asked. "Did you wind up being another scalp on Cole Matthews's belt?"

An uncharacteristic anger flashed through Libbie. "What do you mean?" she asked, ready to lash out at Jill but hoping she'd misunderstood the question.

"Oh, come on, Libbie. I've had my taste of Cole's seductive charm. I know how he operates."

"Do you?" Libbie dropped the stack of files on the corner of Jill's desk. "I've been meaning to ask you about that," she said, her voice so low it hinted at danger. "Just what happened between you and Cole, anyway?"

Jill's expression was one of surprise. "I told you about it before. Nothing more than a little moonlight, a little wine. Another half hour, though, and I might've been another one of his victims. The guy's a manipulator who knows how to take advantage of a situation . . . and a woman's weakness."

Libbie felt the color drain from her face. What Jill was saying simply couldn't be true. "Cole had every opportunity to take advantage of *me* while I was in Washington," she replied, her lips pinched together. "But he didn't."

Jill shrugged. "Maybe by then he didn't have to. You were already infatuated with him."

"Did anybody ever tell you that you're a cynic?" Libbie had rearranged the files in the stack so often during their conversation that now she couldn't remember which ones she wanted to take with her. Sighing in disgust, she started through the stack one more time.

"Frequently." Jill grimaced. "But nobody's perfect. Not me, and not even your wonderful Cole Matthews."

"Jill, do you mind!" Libbie had had enough.

Jill reached toward her In basket and drew out a letter. "If you don't want to talk about it, okay," she said, wanting to make amends. "I didn't realize it was a sore spot with you." She handed Libbie the letter. "I know something is going on, though. Why else would he write and tell *me* he'll be in Austin for the hearings next week? He should've sent the letter to you."

When Libbie entered the Sam Houston Office Building the following week and made her way to the fifth-floor meeting room, it was with a strange sense of déjà vu. Jill was there with many of the same antinuke protesters, and Cole was with the same Pentagon officers who'd been at the initial hearing back in November. The military had made good use of the additional time resulting from the delay, and today they'd added a United States senator and two congressmen from Central Texas to their team. The media were having a field day, and cameras and reporters were everywhere.

Cole carefully avoided Libbie, not even glancing in her direction. When something arose that required communication between the Pentagon and the Coalition, one of the other military officers made the contact.

Libbie's throat was constricted from fighting back tears of disappointment. Even though she and Cole had said their goodbyes in Washington, they'd also declared their love. How can he just ignore me like this? she wondered. If he loves me, why won't he look at me? Has he changed his mind? For her part, she could scarcely keep her eyes off Cole, so great was her soul's hunger to go to him, touch him, clasp him to her heart.

The Pentagon was scheduled to make the first presentation. When the hearing was called to order, Cole described the new safety study that had been conducted and forcefully outlined the changes made in the project design. He then turned over the meeting to his science and engineering experts with their elaborate charts and mock-ups. It was clear to Libbie that the recent changes had resulted in a vastly superior system, and safety conscious though she was, she had a hard time finding flaws in it.

She made a spunky presentation on behalf of the Coalition, but she had the feeling that she was beaten before she'd started. When her team finished, the politicians took the stage with just the right note of powerful leadership and down-home folksiness. Each in turn urged that the nuclear defense project be pushed forward because so much time had already been lost. When one congressman talked about how far behind the United States had fallen, he convinced the mesmerized audience that nothing was more important than catching up with the enemy. When the antinuke protesters heckled him and waved their banners, the rest of the crowd booed them down.

Well, that's that, Libbie thought. We fought like hell, but we lost. All our hard work has come to nothing. She turned and stared out the window at the bleak winter sky. Austin was experiencing a blast of frigid Arctic air, but it couldn't compare with the wintry shards in Libbie's ice-locked heart.

"Today's hearing is adjourned," said the state employee in charge of the meeting. "The final hearing on this project will be conducted in Washington sometime this spring. Watch your local newspaper for the notices."

"I'm getting out of here," Libbie said to Jill. "Thank goodness it's Friday. I'll see you at the office on Monday." She stood and tried to make her way through the crowd before Jill could suggest they go to happy hour somewhere.

Leaving the auditorium was like trying to fight her way upstream, because most of the crowd wanted to go to the front to shake hands with the well-known politicians. Libbie stretched and twisted, trying to create an opening big enough to ease through.

"Looks like you need somebody to run interference for you," said a familiar baritone. By some miracle a wedge opened, and Libbie followed Cole's broad shoulders through the crowd. When they got to the perimeter of the room, he took her hand and steered her to a table where Colonel Jackson stood waiting.

"Hello again, Ms. Greer," said Colonel Jackson, offering his hand. He seemed to be studying Libbie, but his expression was carefully neutral. He handed Cole a paper with typewriting on it. "Here are your orders, Colonel Matthews."

Cole took the paper and flipped it open, then quickly scanned it. "Thank you, sir." He stood at attention and saluted. "I'll see you in Washington on Monday."

"Enjoy your leave," Colonel Jackson replied with the merest trace of a smile. "Don't worry about a thing. I'll take personal charge of your duties."

"Thank you, sir." Cole slowly let out his breath, as if he'd been afraid something had been going to interfere. Then he gave Libbie a bashful, boyish smile that made him look years younger. His fingers locked around her hand in a powerful squeeze. "Let's get out of here," he said.

When they reached the outside hallway, Cole turned to Libbie with a warmth in his eyes that set her pulse to racing.

"Aren't you going to explain?" she asked, stepping out of his reach.

"I've got forty-eight hours' leave," he said. "Go home and pack a suitcase. I'll pick you up in forty-five minutes."

She shook her head, incredulous. "You didn't call me for two months. You didn't even send me a Christmas card. You sent *Jill* a letter telling her you'd be in Austin today for the hearings, but you didn't write *me*. You came in here today and acted like you'd never seen me before. And now all at once you're telling me to go home and pack a suitcase? Are you out of your mind?"

"Probably," he admitted. "I didn't call or write because I couldn't. I can't even tell you where I was assigned temporary duty during those weeks. I wrote Jill instead of you and ignored you in the hearing room because I knew I couldn't have any more official contact with you and still see you privately while I'm here. And I'm telling you to go home and pack a suitcase because I've put the Pentagon in an uproar trying to get forty-eight hours' leave so I could spend it with you. Now, are you going to waste our precious time arguing, or are you going to do what I told you to do?"

"I guess I'm going to spend it arguing." She folded her arms across her chest and tried to look fierce.

"For crying out loud, Libbie." Cole was exasperated. "Do you have any idea how much trouble it was for me to get this leave?"

She lifted her shoulders in an elegant shrug.

"Do you have any idea how hard I've worked making plans for us?"

He was beginning to get her attention. She leaned one elbow against the windowsill and waited to hear more. "Couldn't you have discussed your plans with me? Obviously you've known what you had in mind, but you didn't give me any say in the matter. You didn't even ask me. All you do is bark out your orders and expect me to snap to attention. Well, I'm not in your Army, Colonel Matthews. I'm a civilian."

"How well I know," he muttered. He decided to change his tack. "Libbie, I can't make a move of any kind that isn't planned to the smallest detail weeks or months in advance. And most of the time I'm on top-secret assignments, so I can't contact anyone I know. Every detail of my leave had to be worked out with the Army weeks ago. And getting this leave to spend with you is one of the most foolhardy things I've ever done. I don't know what will happen to us when it's over." He jammed his hands in his pockets and swore under his breath. When he turned back to her his eyes were haunted. "But I couldn't let you go until we had a chance to be together." His voice dropped so low she could scarcely catch his words. "I want to have you for my own, even if it's only for one lousy forty-eight hour leave." He leaned against the windowsill, head down. She could see the muscle twitching at the corner of his jaw. "It's stupid; it's selfish.... But I'm a man, and I love you."

Her heart flip-flopped. He loved her! Libbie reached out to touch his arm. "You know, Cole, we wouldn't waste so much of our precious time if you'd just *ask* once in a while instead of issuing orders."

"Is *that* what you're griping about?" he asked in surprise. "I thought you didn't want to spend the weekend with me."

She leaned against his shoulder and let her hair brush his cheek. "I'm kind of curious about the plans you've made," she said. "After all, if you've spent weeks—"

Cole wrapped his arm around her waist and started down the hallway, drawing her with him. "Let's start with the red roses for an early Valentine's Day gift," he said, whispering into her ear. "And then there's the special French champagne I brought back from one of my trips to Paris." He adjusted his pace so their thighs brushed together in rhythm as they walked. "That's only the beginning," he promised. "That is, if you'll be so kind as to accept my humble invitation?"

Libbie's laughter tinkled like silver bells in a soft summer breeze. "Cole Matthews, you were never *humble* about anything in your life!"

He hugged her against him, then said with teasing candor, "Not until I met you, my darling, not until I met you."

When Cole arrived forty-five minutes later at Libbie's building, he was driving a rented car and dressed in civilian clothes. Left behind at the Bergstrom B.O.Q. were all traces of his military life.

"Wow!" Libbie said, giving him an admiring once-over. "You look great in tight jeans."

"So do you," he said, nuzzling her cheek with his chin.

"Where'd you get the cowboy boots?" she asked.

"What else would a boy from Oklahoma wear on his day off?" Cole asked. He hoisted her travel kit under one elbow and helped her with her coat. "You won't need this coat," he commented. "You're not going to see the light of day for forty-eight hours."

"Promises, promises," Libbie said airily. "Talk's cheap."

He gave her a smoldering look that prickled her skin.

"Would you rather stay here, at my apartment, and start proving yourself right now?" she teased.

Cole shook his head. "I've arranged a special place for us," he said. "On neutral territory. I don't want you to look at your pillow some night and imagine me there."

"Don't you think I've already done that?" Libbie asked, her eyes downcast.

"Have you?" He was surprised to feel such a rush of joy. When they got into the Wagoneer he'd rented, Cole was still smiling.

"Are you addicted to four-wheel drive?" Libbie asked.

"This is a little more luxurious than the Army vehicles you've bounced around in," Cole said, pulling out of her parking lot onto Riverside Drive. "We need four-wheel drive where we're going."

"Where is that, pray tell?" Anticipation was giving Libbie's stomach butterflies.

"Straight up Cat Mountain."

Libbie whistled. "I'd say you've got connections."

He stomped on the accelerator and entered the ramp to the expressway. "I'd say you're right."

It was dark, the moon obscured behind a heavy cloud cover, when they left all the other houses behind and pulled onto a rutted trail leading to their destination, a secluded cabin in the woods. Cole stopped the car, reached for a flashlight in the glove compartment, and as he leaned forward, his shoulder brushed against Libbie's breast. She sighed softly and lifted her face to his.

His heart hammered in his chest, and he bent to kiss her. Her lips were warm and yielding, and he drew them into his mouth, nibbling with his teeth, then tasting with his tongue. She murmured something, then lifted her arms to reach around his neck and draw him closer to her. The heat of desire roused and hardened him, and Libbie seemed to know, for she let her head fall back and parted her lips, drawing his tongue into her mouth, making room for his playful thrusts. The fragrance of lilies-of-the-valley clung to her skin and filled his senses. Little sounds of excitement caught in the back of her throat and made his breathing quicken. He wanted desperately to put his hands on her and caress the lovely curves of her body, but he dared not touch her. His desire was already at the flash point, and he was struggling for control.

Libbie pulled away, breaking the kiss. Her voice wavered, as though she, too, were being lifted in a spiral of passion. "Cole, let's go inside."

He flipped the switch on the flashlight, which blinded them momentarily with its brightness, then opened the car door. Libbie got out of the car while Cole reached in the back for her bag and some other items. "Here," he said hoarsely, "these are for you." He handed her a tissue-wrapped bunch of long-stemmed red roses, and she buried her face in the delicate, spicy-scented blooms. Picking up a wicker picnic basket in one hand and Libbie's bag in the other, Cole juggled things until he could also manage the flashlight and light a path to the cabin. "Careful," he said. "Don't trip over a loose stone." He unlocked the cabin door and threw it open.

A roaring fire, laid by the caretaker a short time earlier, blazed in the stone fireplace that covered one end of the cabin. Enough light was cast by the fire to make shadows dance about the room, creating a sensuous, magical atmosphere. They went inside, and Cole set down the things he was carrying. Libbie walked over to the fireplace and watched the flames. There was no sound except the popping of the fire, the rasp of their breathing.

Libbie turned to face Cole. "Are we really alone?" she asked.

He nodded.

Firelight flickered over Libbie's face, making her eyes sparkle. He leaned against the door, watching her. She was beautiful, with her silky hair cascading in loose curls around her face and across her shoulders. In a few minutes he'd bury his face in her hair and experience its fragrance, something more than soap and fresh air, something totally female. He'd put his hands on her waist, then run them up to cup her full, rounded breasts. Their mouths would cling together in kisses that would make them dizzy. They'd make love, melding bodies and hearts and minds in a perfect fusion of personality. For now they had all the time in the world. His eyes lingered on Libbie. He'd have to rely on a lifetime's training in self-control, but somehow he'd manage to hold himself back so he could lift her to the heights of ecstasy.

Libbie took off her coat and tossed it onto a nearby chair, then reached out her hand and beckoned him to join her at the fire.

"Don't you want a glass of champagne?" Cole asked, walking toward her.

She shook her head. "Later." She opened her arms and Cole stepped into the circle of her love.

Her mouth sought his, and he felt her kisses become a searing liquid, igniting his lips and tongue with hers. She moaned, then strained against him, her body pulsing with an energy that demanded his response. Her fingers dug into his back, and he lifted her against him, locking her pelvis against his. The snaps on their jeans scraped against each other, and her hand moved down to fumble with his zipper.

"Don't, Libbie," he groaned, trying to remove her hand. But she persisted until she'd set him and then herself free from the mechanical impediments that separated them and pushed herself against him.

"Cole, now," she whispered. She dropped onto the thick sheepskin rug in front of the fireplace and pulled him down beside her. She took off her shoes and jeans, then positioned herself, drawing Cole astride her and arching her back.

For weeks he'd planned this moment in his mind, and always he'd wanted to stretch out this time of first lovemaking. But his intentions hadn't taken into account the reality of the woman sighing and straining underneath him. His illusion of self-control burst like the silly bubble it was. The blood roared in his ears, and his body did what it was born to do. His fingers gripped the soft flesh of Libbie's bottom, pulling her up until she opened to him, warm and moist and welcoming, and he thrust himself inside her.

She cried out, then shifted slightly, easing him deeper into her. He felt her tighten around him and thought he would explode from the ecstasy.

"Libbie, don't, sweetheart. I'm losing control."

She paid no heed, and again she arched her back against him. Libbie rotated her hips, sliding against Cole and increasing the exciting friction between them until he responded and drove himself into her again.

This time Cole cried out from the sheer pleasure she was giving him, and when she urged him deeper, he quit fighting for control. Quickly now, with short, eager thrusts, then long, sensual ones, he drove himself into her until their union found its own rhythm and they moved together, faster and faster, until Cole's entire being contracted, then exploded in a fiery burst of passion. The world spun on its axis and Cole was transported....

He had no idea how long it was before his heart slowed its pounding and the orange lights stopped flashing inside his head. When he could speak, he turned to Libbie and pulled her into his arms. "I'm sorry, sweetheart," he said. "This didn't happen the way I'd planned it."

"I wanted you too much. I couldn't wait any longer," she replied.

He rose on one elbow. "But, why? You didn't—I mean, I'm the one who—" There was no way to express himself with any degree of delicacy. He chuckled in embarrassment. "It hasn't been five minutes since we walked in that door. We've still got on some of our clothes. I didn't even have time to kiss you."

Libbie snuggled her head into Cole's shoulder. "Something happens every time we're together," she said. "We never get to be alone, and we're always interrupted. I was afraid you'd get a phone call and have to leave again." She pressed his hand to her lips and kissed the tips of his fingers. "I knew I couldn't bear it if anything happened before we made love. I wanted you to be mine, a part of me, the only way I could have you." Tears of joy sprang to her eyes. She felt an infinite tenderness for Cole and lifted her mouth to kiss his lips.

He clasped her face between his palms and returned her kiss, his mouth moving gently against hers. "I love you, Libbie," he whispered. "I've never known anyone like you." He shifted so that her body lay below him, and he leaned down to kiss her again with a growing pressure. She felt his hands slip underneath her sweater, and then he found her breasts. She sighed with pleasure as he fondled her, caressing her until her nipples began to tingle. In a deft motion he pulled the sweater over her head, then unfastened her bra and tossed it aside.

The firelight played over her bare torso, illuminating her silken curves. Libbie lay still, watching Cole as his eyes assaulted her. He couldn't seem to take his eyes from her breasts, and he reached out to toy with her nipple until it stiffened. He smiled at her body's eager response, then returned to repeat the tantalizing motion on her other breast. She stretched languidly, enjoying the erotic sensations that spread outward from the tips of her breasts. Her arm lifted, slipped underneath his shoulder to pull down his head, and then she twisted so that he could bury his face in the sweetness of her bosom.

Cole began to kiss her cheeks, the hollow of her throat, her eyelids, his mouth never stopping its journey of pleasure. He slipped one hand between her legs and began to stroke the velvety warmth until she moaned softly and put her hand over his to increase the urgent sensation she was experiencing. Cole bent to her breasts, taking turns with each nipple, drawing it fully into his mouth, licking its outer circle, then nibbling with his teeth until her breathing was ragged.

"Cole," she whispered, wanting more than he was giving her.

When the pressure of his mouth increased, her body became a torch of desire, and she arched her back, thrashing against the bewitching sensuality of his mouth and hands. Her fingers dug into his shoulders, and she felt the rough wool of his sweater against her bare skin.

He shifted and pulled off his sweater, then the rest of his clothing, and kicked it out of the way. He lay beside her, his chest hard and bronzed in the firelight, his shoulders and biceps fully developed from a lifetime of calisthenics.

"Your body is beautiful," Libbie said in awe. She reached out to touch the hard, flat planes of his abdomen, then let her fingers trail downward. He sprang to life underneath her touch, and Libbie gasped.

Cole lay flat on his back and pulled Libbie on top, her head and torso suspended above him, her breasts swaying above his chin. He reached up and caught her nipple between his teeth. He tugged gently until she let herself drop. His hands slid down the curve of her back, over her buttocks, and with a swift jerk he joined their bodies and thrust upward, entering her.

Libbie controlled their rhythm, lifting herself, then sliding downward with urgent strokes. Cole tangled his fingers in her hair, drawing her closer to him so he could kiss her again and again, his tongue invading her mouth to the same raging cadence that propelled their fused bodies. His hands found her breasts and cupped them, tracing their curves and hollows until she felt herself melting outward from the center. She let out a cry, and as one they rolled over until Cole was above her, driving himself into her, thrusting into her quivering darkness until her passion burst like a cascade of exploding rockets, carrying her to the edge of the universe and the blue-white star of pure sensation.

Chapter Ten

The warmth of the fire wrapped Libbie and Cole in a lovers' cocoon, lulling them as they lay in each other's arms.

"I love you," Cole whispered.

"I know," Libbie replied, her voice full of wonder. For now, that was enough. Monday would be soon enough to face the reality that their lives were spinning in separate orbits. She reached for the red roses, which had been forgotten and crushed during their tempestuous lovemaking. "I'll never smell roses again without remembering this moment," Libbie said softly, taking one of the flowers and crumbling its petals over Cole's chest.

The scent invaded their nostrils, and Cole took another bloom and scattered its petals in Libbie's hair. "I love the smell of your hair," he said. "And the feel of it, like silk through my fingers." He caressed a shiny chestnut coil, then bent to kiss it, his breath a soft breeze against her ear.

"That tickles," she said, giggling. Her fingers toyed with the rose petals strung across Cole's chest until he chuckled. "Are you ticklish, too?" she asked. Her lips followed the rose petals, tracing tiny kisses across his skin.

He smiled down at her. "Yes, I'm ticklish. And I'm also hungry. A man's got to have food if he's going to keep up such a vigorous pace."

"But you were a Green Beret," Libbie replied, moving against him in a sensual gesture that was meant to tease more than to arouse. "You're supposed to be able to do a thirty-mile forced march without even breathing hard." She lifted herself on one elbow so that the firelight shimmered on her bare breasts.

Cole caressed her satiny skin. "Well, if you insist—" With a wicked gleam in his eye he pulled her down beside him and threw one leg across hers.

Libbie laughed into his shoulder. "Never mind," she said. "I'm hungry, too. What's in that picnic basket you brought?"

"It used to be chateaubriand and wild rice from Green Mansions restaurant," he answered. "I imagine it's now become dried-out beef jerky." He sat up and grinned at Libbie. "That'll teach you to mess around with a schedule that's been planned with military precision." He pulled Libbie up onto her knees and into his arms. "Come on, sweetheart. Let's go take a shower and then I'll give you a sample of Army KP."

When they switched on the lights, Libbie discovered that what in the darkness had appeared to be a simple log cabin was instead a luxurious mountain lodge, with every amenity wealth could buy. She and Cole showered together in a double-sized shower with built-in ledges and clear glass doors. Adjoining was a redwood compartment containing a Finnish sauna, where they parched for five minutes in the steam of heated rocks. They finished up with a leisurely, relaxing soak in a whirlpool tub. When Cole tried to pull Libbie to her feet and dry her with a velvety towel, she collapsed on the lush carpeting and gestured him away.

"I'm too limp to move," she said. "Wake me when it's morning."

"You're not getting off that easy." He playfully whacked her fanny with the towel. "Come on, let me dry you off."

"In a minute," Libbie said, rolling over to make room for him beside her. "It's shameless of me, but I enjoy looking at your naked body here in the light."

"Aren't you going to do anything besides look?" he said, his grin cocky enough to let her know he was back in business. He lay down beside Libbie and let her run her fingers over his skin.

She found a scar on his shoulder she hadn't noticed before. "What's this?" she asked.

"Sniper bullet." He caught her fingers in his hand and moved them to his chest, as though he wanted to put an end to her curiosity.

Libbie lifted her head and kissed the scar. "Aren't you going to tell me about it?"

He shook his head. "You're beautiful," he whispered. His forefinger reached out to trace the line of her eyebrow, then curved down her cheekbone trifle with her mouth.

She parted her lips and nipped at his finger with her teeth. "There's so much I don't know about you," she whispered. "I'm jealous of all those years of your life before I met you." She didn't add the painful corollary that she was jealous of the years ahead when his life would go on without her.

"Don't be jealous," Cole replied. "Those years shaped me and made me what I am. If I hadn't experienced all the things I have, I wouldn't have the capacity to love you the way I do." His finger found a dimple at the corner of her lips and brushed it with a feathery touch. "I never knew what true joy was until tonight."

She drew him into a loving embrace. As her hands moved across his back, she felt a strange aberration in his skin that she'd noticed earlier, when they'd been making love by the fireplace. She shifted her position so she could see Cole's back. In the bright bathroom light, the cluster of circular scars was grisly. "How did this happen?" she asked in a shocked voice.

"Cigarette burns. I was captured by the Viet Cong for a few days." Cole turned away, hiding the sight from her view, and moved her hands over his unblemished chest. "Touch this part of me," he insisted.

Her fingers moved with a gossamer touch over the ridges and hollows of his chest, then down his abdomen and across his hips. Libbie's mouth followed the trail marked by her fingers. She moved so her mouth could continue its journey across the solid bone of his hip, then up his waist and against his back. Her lips found the darkened pigment of each burn mark and gently kissed it. Her fingers continued to stroke and knead his shoulders while she kissed the scars, and his skin became damp with her tears.

"Hey," he said, turning over and drawing her face to his.

"I love you, Cole," she said, her eyes moist.

Their lips met. Cole's mouth moved delicately, slowly, over Libbie's while he encircled her cheeks with his palms. Somehow, magically, it was a kiss with all the tenderness of youth and first love, of spring days and moonlit nights. It was the kiss that would have been theirs if they'd met long ago, before life scarred them and robbed them of their innocence. It was the kiss of a love so pure and true and right that fate decreed it should be theirs, even if only for a few snatched hours. When the kiss ended, they both knew they'd never be the same again.

If their salad was a little wilted and their beef tenderloin a little dry, they didn't care. They held hands across a candle-lit table, gazing into each other's eyes, and satisfied the soul's hunger for reciprocated love. Cole perked a pot of strong black coffee to go with a rich dessert made of pastry, pecans, and creamy chocolate. Afterward they sat on the floor beside the fire and sipped champagne from stemmed crystal glasses.

"To the most wonderful woman in the world," Cole said, offering a toast.

"And to the man of her dreams," Libbie replied, snuggling against him. Soft music played on the stereo, and firelight flickered against the ceiling. A mantel clock with Westminster chimes pealed the hour.

"Eleven o'clock." Cole automatically checked his watch, set for Eastern time. "It's midnight in Washington."

"Are you sleepy?" Libbie asked. She sipped the last of her champagne.

"Um-hm. But I don't want to waste any of our time sleeping," Cole answered. He turned up the music. "Let's go out on the deck and dance." When he opened the back door, a wintry gust of wind pelted them. He wrapped Libbie in her short coat and shrugged into his own walnut-brown leather jacket. "I thought you told me Austin winters were so mild you didn't need a coat."

"Usually you don't," she answered. "But this is February. Even in Austin you need a coat after the sun goes down."

"The air smells damp," Cole said, holding out his arms to Libbie. "Come dance with me and keep me warm."

They danced under the starless sky, their only illumination the shaft of light coming through the window of the lodge. Far below them they could see the lights of the city twinkling in the darkness. The lodge itself was secluded by live oak trees, cedar, and a few pines that filled the night with their pungent fragrance. Libbie and Cole danced on and on, lost in their own private, enchanted world.

The cassette recording ended, and they went back inside the lodge to start a new one. "How about another bite of dessert while we're here?" Cole asked.

Libbie uttered a merry laugh. "You and that sweet tooth of yours," she teased. "I still say you're going to get fat and then nobody will want you."

"Not even you?"

"Heavens, no," she said, giving him a coy smile. "I'm only interested in that magnificent body of yours."

"I'm disillusioned." Cole popped the cork on another bottle of champagne and poured Libbie a fresh glass. "Here, you drink and I'll eat," he said. He lifted his sweater to be sure he didn't have any excess flab around the middle, then cut himself another piece of dessert.

"Go ahead, stuff yourself," Libbie said. "The Army will always want you, even if no one else does."

"Not if I get fat. They'd make me retire." Cole took a bite of his dessert and smiled blissfully as he swallowed it. "There must be at least a thousand calories in every bite," he said, sighing.

Libbie gave him a reflective look. "Would the Army really make you retire?" she asked.

"Sure, if I don't stay physically fit. I've got my twenty years in. I can retire anytime." He offered her a bite of his dessert. "This is delicious," he said. "Don't you want some of it?"

She shook her head. "Have you ever thought about retiring from the Army?" she asked.

"Not for a New York minute." He reached out to grip her wrist. "Libbie, don't start trying to plan some kind of future for us. The Army is my life. I thought you understood that."

"I do." She lowered her lashes. "How is it that you can always read my mind?" she asked.

"Because you don't know how to hide your feelings, sweetheart. It doesn't take a genius to know you're thinking that if I retired from the Army, maybe we could find a way to be together." His voice became gentle. "Don't torment yourself with an impossible dream, Libbie."

She turned her hand, palm upward in his and looked at him with wide eyes. "Is it impossible, when we love each other?"

"Can you give up your work in the peace movement?" Cole's question was a blunt instrument, hacking at Libbie's illusions.

She shook her head. She didn't even have to think about her answer. Working toward world peace was the whole purpose of her life.

"You see?" Cole gave her a searching glance. "I can't give up my life's work any more than you can give up yours. I'd shrivel up and die inside." His laughter was mocking. "I don't know what drives me this way," he said, reaching to draw her into his arms. "Any normal man would grab you and run. I think I must be crazy in the head."

"Let's don't talk about it anymore," Libbie said. "It'll only spoil the time we have left." She lifted her lips for his kiss. "Hey, soldier," she whispered. "Don't you think it's time for bed?"

Libbie woke in Cole's arms to a world that seemed unusually bright. She stirred to discover him watching her. "I thought you'd never wake up," he said, kissing her good morning. "It snowed last night."

"It snowed?" Libbie sat bolt upright in bed and looked out the patio doors to see everything lightly dusted with white. "It snowed one time last year," she said. "How exciting!"

"Maybe we'll be snowed in for the rest of the winter," Cole said lazily, burrowing his face into her neck.

"No such luck. It'll melt by noon." She threw back the covers. "Come on, soldier, we've got to hurry and get dressed."

They showered together, but when their bodies were slick with lather and Cole tried to nudge Libbie into the corner of the stall, she laughed and pushed him away. "Time's a-wasting," she said.

"My sentiments exactly," he complained, reaching for her again.

"The snow, Cole, the snow." Libbie was like a child on Christmas morning, greedy to indulge herself in nature's unexpected gift.

"You really are a California girl, aren't you?" he said, smiling indulgently at her. "Nobody else would get so excited about half an inch of snow." He splashed her to rinse off the soap, then toweled her dry and wrapped the towel around her hips, leaving her breasts bare. He dug around in his duffel bag for a clean shirt and underwear and found a tissue-wrapped parcel. "In all the excitement last night, I forgot to give this to you," he said.

"What is it?" Libbie asked in surprise.

"Just a little something I picked up." He watched her face while she tore away the tissue and discovered an angora sweater the color of pistachio ice cream.

She lifted the sweater from the folds of paper and held it in front of her. The color emphasized the green flecks in her eyes and added mysterious depths to them. "Cole, it's beautiful," she said. "But don't you know you're spoiling me?"

"For forty-eight hours I want to spoil the hell out of you," he said huskily. "Put it on and see if it fits."

Libbie lifted her arms, and Cole eased the sweater down over her bare torso. It clung to her breasts and waist, and Cole reached out to touch her.

"So soft," he murmured.

"The angora?"

"The woman inside it." He cleared his throat. "I think I'd better go cook breakfast while you blow-dry your hair," he said. "Otherwise, the snow isn't the only thing around here that's going to melt."

They took a long walk after breakfast and followed animal tracks into the woods. A hawk soared overhead, searching the snow for its prey. A ground squirrel scurried to safety when Libbie and Cole got too close, and across the road they saw a doe with her fawn. A twig broke underneath Libbie's foot, and the doe lifted her head, startled by an intruder in the peaceful woods. In a flash both mother and baby deer were gone from sight.

Cole bent over and scooped up a handful of snow, then chucked it at Libbie. It burst with a soft plopping sound, and she laughed, then made a snowball and tossed it at Cole. Soon they were engaged in an all-out snowball fight, but Cole managed to stay beyond Libbie's throwing range most of the time so that he landed more direct hits than she did.

"Not fair," she complained. "I didn't spend my youth chucking rocks at fruit jars."

"Admit the truth," Cole retorted, shouting across the combat zone. "Males have superior strength and better muscle development. That's why we can throw better."

"Not so," she insisted. "You've just had more experience."

A snowball hit her right in the middle of her nose. She bent over to make another one, and Cole made a toss that pelted her fanny dead center. She hurried to get her pitch in the air, but he was upon her, running across the combat zone and bombarding her with one snowball after another. "Surrender!" he called, tackling her and pulling her down to the ground.

"Surrender, hell!" she retorted, grabbing a handful of snow and stuffing it down his open collar. "I've still got plenty of fight left in me."

She reached for another handful of snow, but Cole was on top of her, his grip so tight on her wrist she couldn't move it. With his other hand he mashed a snowball onto her cheek.

"Surrender," he said again, sitting astride her with a devilish glint in his eye.

"Surrender or what?" she asked. There was something exciting about the way he was looking at her.

He forced a handful of snow into the open vee of her sweater. "Surrender or be buried alive in a snowbank."

Crystals of snow began to melt against the warmth of her skin and trickle down her neck. "Where are you going to find a snowbank in half an inch of snow?"

Cole lifted her sweater and crumbled a snowball onto her bare breasts, then grinned when her nipples puckered from the shock. "What an interesting reaction," he commented, her question forgotten.

Libbie blushed. "You'd pucker up, too, if someone did that to you."

"Want to try it?" He formed a snowball and placed it in her hand. "I'm all yours," he said, his eyes narrowed with a sudden rush of desire.

"I thought you wanted me to surrender," Libbie teased.

"Now I'm more interested in negotiating a truce. Something that'll be for our . . . *mutual* benefit."

Libbie swallowed hard. "Out here in the snow, you mean?"

"You aren't cold, are you?"

She shook her head. "No."

Cole took off his jacket and lifted Libbie long enough to lay it underneath her hair. "That'll keep you dry so you won't catch cold," he said. He trailed another shower of snowflakes over her breasts, then bent to warm her puckered nipples with his tongue.

"My turn," she said, unbuttoning his shirt and rubbing his chest with the snowball he'd given her. He shivered, and she giggled when his tiny male nipples puckered. "It's hard to tell with you," she joshed. "You don't have much equipment."

"My endowments are elsewhere," he replied, then realized too late the consequences of his statement. "No, Libbie. No. Absolutely not." He tried to meld his pelvis against hers, but her hand crept in between and found his zipper. "Libbie, no!"

Her snowball found its target, and he let out a blood-curdling scream.

"My goodness, you really are a Cherokee Indian, aren't you?" she said, smiling sweetly at him. "Please be quiet before you frighten the deer."

"You've ruined me for life," he groaned, writhing above her. "All those years I fought with my helmet covering my privates, and here you've caught me with no protection and destroyed me forever with a snowball."

"Are you sure the damage is permanent?" she inquired, chuckling. "I would've sworn—" She reached down to check. "Oh, poor baby," she cooed. "What a shame."

Cole flopped over on his back, his head beside hers on the jacket. "You broke it," he said glumly. "So you can just fix it."

"I'll try," Libbie said softly, "but of course I can't make any guarantees." She reached out to touch him, stroking gently and warming him with her own heat. His reaction was immediate. "I believe your battery is okay," she said, smiling at him. "You just needed a little jump start."

"For all I know, I've got a burnt-out cell in my battery, and when I cut off the motor, I'll never get it started again."

"Then maybe you better keep the engine running." Libbie drew his head to her breasts and adjusted her sweater, offering him her nipple. His mouth closed on the rosy stem and suckled it to full, throbbing arousal. Soon the hush of the woods was broken by the soft moans of two lovers, each intent on giving the other the ultimate in passion, the ultimate in completeness. The snow melted long before their desire was spent.

Their time flew past, though they tried to make the most of every precious minute. Early Sunday afternoon they both became very quiet, knowing that the time of parting was imminent. Cole had to report to Bergstrom AFB at six o'clock to hop a flight to Washington. They would have to leave the lodge by four.

Libbie lay with her head on Cole's lap while he thumbed through a magazine. "Aren't you going to tell me about your daughter?'' she asked. ''I've wondered about her.''

He looked down at her in surprise. ''Have you? Why?''

''Because she's part of your life that I don't know about. Do you have a picture of her?''

Cole shook his head. ''I never carry anything with me except my orders and whatever currency I need. It's a precaution in case—''

In case something happens to him, Libbie thought. His work is more dangerous than I realized. And he doesn't want to talk about it. ''Tell me what she looks like.''

''She's almost fourteen and very tiny, like her mother. Very beautiful, like her mother. But stubborn and unhappy sometimes, and her mother wasn't like that at all.'' Cole sighed. His daughter, Lai, was often a mystery to him.

''Where does she live?'' Libbie asked. ''Surely not with you.''

''Lord, no. What would I do with her? I'm never home.'' He rumpled Libbie's hair. ''She stays with my folks in Oklahoma. They love her and do the best they can for her. I stop off there when I'm traveling west, and Lai comes to Washington for a week now and then when she's out of school.''

''Why is she unhappy?'' Libbie could visualize the child, caught up in a civil war, her mother dead, living with strangers in Holland for two years, then going to live with other strangers in Oklahoma. She must have experienced a lot of tragedy and change for someone so young.

''Who knows? I don't know how to talk to her. Most of the time I feel like a stranger with her.'' His hand formed a fist and pounded the palm of his other hand. "I'm no good at being a father," Cole said. "I never meant to have a child."

Libbie got up on her knees to listen. "Why not?"

"Because of the war. I knew there was a good chance I'd be killed, and I didn't want to leave a widow behind with a child to take care of. But Nguyet was determined to have a baby. She said if I got killed, she wanted part of me to live on." Cole leaned his head against the back of the sofa and shuddered. "Instead it was Nguyet who was killed, and Lai is the part of *her* that lives on. It would break Nguyet's heart if she knew how I'd failed her daughter."

"How have you failed her?" Cole's pain was obvious to Libbie, yet there seemed no good reason for it.

"By not making room for her in my life." His voice was flat and empty. "I tell myself she's happier in Oklahoma than she'd be with me, but deep down I know it's not true. She wants to be with me, and she doesn't understand why it's impossible." He shook his head. He couldn't talk about it anymore. Lai was the part of his life that he'd botched.

Libbie lifted Cole's hand to her lips and kissed his palm. "What was your wife like? Nguyet," she said, stumbling over the pronunciation, which was something like "noo YET."

"Beautiful. Brave."

"Did you love her very much?" There was an icy lump of fear in Libbie's throat.

"Oh, yes," Cole said softly. "Very much. I loved Nguyet the way a boy loves at nineteen, when he's rash and full of fire. The war intensified all that, and Nguyet was always there to welcome me back from dangerous missions. She was a simple village girl who gave her love and asked nothing in return.'' He scooped Libbie into his arms. ''But I didn't love her the way I love you, my darling. I was only a boy then, and she was only a girl. That love was sweet, but it didn't compare with the love of a mature man and woman.'' He bent his head and kissed Libbie, fully and passionately.

She sighed and twisted her arms around his neck. Gone was any lingering jealousy of his first love. Her lips parted.

Cole lifted his wrist so he could see his watch. ''It's almost time to leave,'' he said. ''Do you think we have time—''

''If we hurry,'' Libbie answered.

Chapter Eleven

Cole sat in Colonel Jackson's office on the third floor of the Pentagon, giving additional details to go with the written report of his most recent trip to Western Europe.

"So you think there may be some problems in Germany?" the colonel asked, peering at Cole over the top of his reading glasses.

"Yes, sir. And in the Scandinavian countries as well. The Chernobyl disaster has made everybody jumpy." Cole handed his commanding officer a sheaf of telexes and another set of coded reports.

"Does it seem to be a matter of political opportunism?" Colonel Jackson leaned back in his oversized chair and drummed the desk with his fingers, deep in thought.

"No, sir, not in any large measure. I think everybody is concerned about human safety. Issues that used to be theoretical have become dramatically real, and government leaders everywhere are worried. What if there's another reactor failure? What if the meltdown can't be stopped the next time? Is the China Syndrome a legitimate possibility? Those are the questions everybody is asking.''

"Safety." Colonel Jackson mulled over the issue. "That's the bandwagon everybody is jumping on. Including that Coalition down in Texas. We've had to do a lot of redesigning to try to get congressional approval of our nuclear defense proposal, and we still have a long way to go." The colonel got up, walked over to the window and stared out at the huge parking lot below.

"We've come up with a better system, though," Cole said quietly. "The time and money were well spent."

Colonel Jackson turned to face Cole. "Whose side are you on, anyway?" he asked with a mirthless laugh.

Cole exhaled with a soft whoosh of breath. "The Army's, of course. But we're obligated to give the American people the safest weapons system we can."

Cole massaged his temple to ease a gnawing pain. The colonel's question was one that Cole had asked himself all too often in the past six weeks. *Whose side are you on, anyway?* Libbie had forced Cole to take a broad look at the nuclear issue, and he'd had to admit that some of her points were well taken. But the broad view was detrimental to his effectiveness as a Pentagon officer assigned to development of nuclear projects. The most effective officer was one with a severe case of tunnel vision, one who set his sights on a goal and let nothing deter his progress toward it. Life had been much simpler for Cole in the old days, before Libbie, when he'd taken the specialist's approach to his work.

"Do you have a headache?" Colonel Jackson asked, noticing Cole's fingers at his temple.

"No, sir, just a little jet lag."

"We've been pushing you pretty hard," Colonel Jackson admitted. "How many trips have you made to Europe lately?"

"Since my leave in February, I've made six. One every week."

"That's too much for one person," the colonel said, going back to his desk. "You're tough enough to handle it, but we need to be training someone else. Don't we have somebody with a top-secret security clearance we can break in?"

The two men considered other officers who might be available and came up with several names.

"I'll get to work on selecting someone right away," Colonel Jackson said. "It just dawned on me that there's nobody but you to handle this area. If anything happened to you, I'd have to take over your responsibilities myself. And God knows *I* don't want to go to Europe every week. How do you stand the grind?"

Cole gave a rueful chuckle. "It's my job. I'm following orders."

"Don't you ever wish for another kind of duty, though—say, commander of a military base in Hawaii or someplace where it's always warm?"

"Sometimes lately I've wished I could have some kind of private life," Cole conceded. "But I couldn't stand being put out to pasture. The war against oppression never gets any easier. We still have to fight it one day at a time, and I'm a soldier. That's the battle I've chosen."

The colonel gave Cole a calculating look and ignored the philosophical statement he'd just made, instead zeroing in on his remark about his private life. The two men had worked together for several years, and never had Cole made a single complaint about responsibilities that would overwhelm anybody else. He wasn't complaining now, either, but Colonel Jackson had caught the wistful note in Cole's voice.

"This recent contemplation of your private life wouldn't have anything to do with that pretty young gal from Texas, would it?" Colonel Jackson was sympathetic. Libbie Greer was the kind of woman to get under a man's skin.

Cole sighed. "Yes, sir, I'm afraid it does."

"Hell, Cole, you joined the Army, not the priesthood. The Army doesn't expect you to stay single the rest of your life."

"I know that." Cole shook his head. "I just haven't happened to meet anybody else I've wanted to marry. And with Libbie, marriage wouldn't work. How can I fly around the country doing my job for the Army and have her on the next plane picketing everything I do?"

Colonel Jackson laughed. As a third party, he could afford to be amused. "I can see how it might create a few problems for you," he agreed.

"Not just for me, Colonel. She'd create problems for the Army, too."

"You don't think she'd compromise your security clearance, do you?" National security was the most sensitive of all issues, and Cole's head was full of information that must never be divulged to an unauthorized person.

"Oh, no, that's not what I meant." Cole spread his hand in a mute appeal. "She's completely above board. It's that she's opposed to almost everything the military tries to do. She's not a simple antinuclear activist, Colonel. She's involved in the world peace movement. She's a pacifist."

The colonel whistled. "A soldier and a pacifist. What an intriguing combination. Well, Cole, looks to me like you've got your work cut out for you."

"What's that, sir?"

"Trying to figure out some way to accommodate your separate goals."

Cole stood and jammed his hands in his pockets. "That's just it, sir. There's no way to do that."

"Don't be so sure until you give it a try." The colonel stood and put an arm across Cole's shoulder. "You're a good officer, son. The Army's more flexible than you realize when it comes to the special needs of its best and brightest." He walked Cole to the door. "Go give that gal a call and get her up here for a week or so. See how she fits into your life. Let her get acquainted with your daughter and with some officers' wives. Then we'll talk again."

"But, sir," Cole protested, looking down at the orders in his hand. "I've already told my daughter she couldn't come during spring break, because I have to go to France. We've got to start laying the groundwork for the upcoming NATO meeting."

The colonel sighed. He'd make the supreme sacrifice. He took Cole's orders and ripped them into pieces. "I'll go to Paris for you," he said, forcing a smile. "Maybe their winter's almost over."

* * *

The tension in Cole's apartment was incredible. By careful planning, he'd arranged to get Libbie and Lai to Washington during the first week of April, both arriving by commercial flights on Friday afternoon. Since this was a personal visit, not official, there'd be no military flights or chauffeurs and no Concord House lodging for Libbie this trip.

Lai had her usual room in Cole's two-bedroom Arlington apartment, and he'd given his own room to Libbie and planned to bunk on the couch himself. Cole knew it wouldn't do to share a bedroom with Libbie while his daughter was there. It would be enough if Lai and Libbie could get acquainted, without complicating the situation any further.

Still, he'd thought the three of them would be able to do some sight-seeing and make the first efforts to develop a relationship. He'd thought the big problem of the visit would be trying to work out his differences with Libbie over their conflicting careers. But he'd thought wrong. He hadn't reckoned on his daughter's bad humor.

"Should I go in and try to talk to her?" Libbie asked, sitting on the edge of the sofa, ill at ease.

Cole was embarrassed over his daughter's behavior and angry that she'd put him in such an uncomfortable position. How could she be rude to their guest and storm off to her room, refusing to go to dinner? The visit had just begun, and already Cole was wondering how the three of them could stay under one roof for an entire week.

"I'll go see if I can find out what the problem is," Cole said, ruffling Libbie's silky hair. He wanted to take her in his arms and kiss her, really kiss her, but as sure as he did, Lai would walk in on them. He and Libbie would have no privacy this visit, and his body's hunger for her was something else he'd underestimated.

He walked slowly down the hallway to Lai's closed bedroom door and took a deep breath, then rapped. It was a firm, masculine knock that sounded more confident than Cole felt. "Lai?" he said when she didn't answer. "Lai, I'm coming in to talk to you." He gave her a few seconds, then opened the door.

Lai sat staring out the window, her chin in her palms, and refused to turn around to look at Cole. Her entire bearing projected outrage. Cole walked over and put his hand on her shoulder.

She flinched at his touch and jerked away. "Leave me alone," she said.

She was taller than when he'd seen her last, several months earlier, but her body was as delicate and fine-boned as ever. Her hair and eyes were dark, and her skin was creamy in the way of Amerasians. She wore a loose-knit sweater and slacks outfit that was the pale pink of rosebuds and made her look dainty and feminine and vulnerable. Cole felt a stirring of fatherly pride in her beauty and tried again to show his affection by putting his arm around her.

"Can't you give your dad a hug?" he asked, trying to be patient with her.

She shook her head. "Why did you let me come when you've got *her* here?" she said angrily. "I wish I'd stayed home with Grandma and Grandpa."

Cole squatted down on his knees so their faces would be at the same level. "I wanted you to get to know Libbie," he said. "That's why I asked you both to come at the same time. I hope you'll be friends."

"Why? Are you going to marry her?" Lai's dark eyes, which were neither slanted nor round but a bewitching almond shape, filled with tears.

"We don't know yet whether we're going to get married. We've been thinking about it, but there are a lot of problems we'll have to work out first."

Lai lowered her face into her hands and let hot, stinging tears fall down her cheeks. "You wouldn't let *me* come to Washington to live with you," she sobbed. "You said you were too busy with your job."

Cole reached out to take Lai's hands, at an absolute loss to know what to say. He found his handkerchief and dabbed at her tears.

"How can you have time for *her*, since you never had time for *me*?" Lai raged.

"Lai, shh, she'll hear you. You don't want to hurt Libbie's feelings."

"I don't care if she hears me. You've been hurting my feelings for years. Why should I care about *her* feelings?" Lai took the handkerchief and blew her nose. "Can I go home tomorrow? I don't want to stay with you anymore."

"You won't give me another chance?" he asked.

Lai vigorously shook her head. "I don't need you anyway. I've got Grandma and Grandpa. They want me."

Cole sat down on the floor with his knees bent and buried his face in his folded arms. Her words had been like a rapier, piercing his heart in one cruel thrust. "You can leave tomorrow if you wish," he said in a flat voice when he could get enough breath to speak. "I wouldn't want you to stay against your will."

"I want to leave. I'll call Grandma and tell her I'm coming home." Lai didn't look up as Cole got to his feet and slowly walked to the door. When he shut it behind him, she buried her face in her hands and wept.

When Cole walked back into the living room, Libbie got up and came to him. "I'm sorry," she said, putting her arms around him.

"I guess you heard everything she said." Cole rested his chin on the crown of Libbie's head and let his arms loosely enfold her.

"She's little, but she's loud," Libbie said, trying to ease the tension with a smile.

"I told you I'd failed at being a father," Cole said, gritting his teeth in despair. "I've never been able to talk to her. Every visit ends up in an argument." He tilted Libbie's face, searching for the love in her eyes. "It's never been this bad before, though. She's never demanded to go back to Oklahoma as soon as she got here."

"Are you really going to let her go?" Libbie could sense the child's pain as well as Cole's. Running away was no answer.

"What else can I do? She wants to go, and if I make her stay, she'll ruin the trip for you, too."

"If you let her go, you're going to lose her forever," Libbie said gently. "If you really want to be a father to her, you're going to have to do it now."

"How can I be a father to her? She won't let me!" Frustration rose in Cole, and he left Libbie and went onto the patio to stare out across the hillside.

Libbie followed him outdoors, knowing she was pushing him too hard, knowing it had to be done. She reached for his hand and gripped it. "You're a soldier, Cole, and this is a battle. If you stand back and keep your distance, you'll give her room to get at her weapons. She'll hurt you and break your heart, because that's what she thinks you've done to her."

The current of their love flowed between their linked hands. "I didn't know you were a war tactician," Cole said, trying to smile. "Tell me, General, what's my best move?"

"Don't laugh at me," Libbie said, standing on tiptoe to brush his lips with hers.

"I won't. Just help me, Libbie, if you can. I don't want to lose her."

"You're going to have to move in so close she doesn't have room to fight you," Libbie answered. "You're going to have to wrap your arms around her and squeeze her and love her until all the fight's gone out of her." Their eyes met. "It isn't going to be easy," Libbie added.

"About as easy as hugging a porcupine," Cole replied. The lopsided grin he gave Libbie was genuine. She'd given him his first hope that things with Lai could improve.

"You'll have to be as patient as you are when you're trying to reel in a congressman's vote on one of your military projects."

Cole kissed Libbie's hand. "I can manage that. Anything else?"

"You might as well get started. Go back in there and find out where she wants to go for dinner tonight."

Cole felt himself grow weak in the knees. The theory sounded fine, but suddenly, having to put it into practice intimidated him. How was he going to hug a child who stiffened at his touch? "Do you think maybe she'd listen to you?" he asked, hoping Libbie could take the first step for him.

"Coward," she scolded. "You've got to do this yourself, Cole. I'm an intruder, and she resents the hell out of me."

"She resents me, too."

"Yes," Libbie said gently. "But she also loves you. Go in there and convince her that you love her even more."

If there was some slight improvement in matters between Cole and his daughter, things continued to deteriorate between Lai and Libbie. Lai's jealousy was put on offensive display, though she saved her most hateful behavior for times when Cole wasn't around to see it. Sometimes it was all Libbie could do to keep from grabbing Lai by the shoulders and giving her a good shake. She had to remind herself constantly that the child had good reason to be unhappy and confused and that the only way to change her behavior was through love.

It was easier said than done.

Cole, however, seemed encouraged, because there were times when Lai did respond to him with something more than sullen indifference. She took great pains with her appearance because Cole's pride in her beauty was so easy to detect. He complimented her pretty dresses and the way she wore her long black hair. He took her shopping and bought her a delicate gold chain for her neck and generally tried to express his love in the only way he knew how, by indulging her with presents.

The situation got tricky when he tried to buy a gift for Libbie as well. Lai got in such a snit that Cole abandoned the diamond-studded earrings he'd been admiring in the jeweler's case. It wasn't fair to Libbie to make her play second fiddle to a bratty teenager, though Libbie herself had the patience and understanding of a saint and took the situation in stride. Nonetheless, Cole felt himself torn asunder by the two females he loved and wondered whether the time would ever come when the three of them could be together without stress and turmoil.

"You're going to get an afternoon off," he said to Libbie at breakfast the following Friday morning while Lai was in the bathroom doing her hair and they had a few minutes' privacy. "The circus is in town, and a bunch of officers' kids are going together. I got a ticket for Lai so you could have a break."

Libbie couldn't hold back a smile of relief. It had been a long, hard week for her. "Are you going to be free this afternoon?" she asked. How wonderful it would be if they could spend an afternoon alone together.

Cole reached across the table to grip her hand. "I wish I were," he said, hunger in his eyes. "We'd rent the ritziest room at the Mayflower Hotel and hang a Do Not Disturb sign on the door."

Libbie lowered her eyes to conceal her disappointment. With Colonel Jackson doing Cole's stint in Paris, Cole had to go to the Pentagon every day to monitor their section as well as train his new assistant. Most days, though, he'd been able to get away from the office for a few hours to accompany Libbie and Lai sight-seeing and shopping.

"We're expecting a military attaché from one of the Middle East countries," Cole explained. "I've got to be there and show my assistant the ropes."

Libbie nodded. "It's okay," she said. "There are lots of things I've been wanting to do that would only bore Lai. I'll take advantage of the time to myself."

"Are you sure that's what you want to do?" Cole asked. "Colonel Jackson's wife is having some kind of bridge party and tea this afternoon, and she's going to call and invite you to come. You don't have to go, though. It's up to you."

"I haven't played bridge in a long time," Libbie said. "Not since college. I never seem to have time for things like that anymore."

"I don't think there's as much bridge playing as there is gossip. The bridge is only an excuse to get together and discuss why someone didn't get promoted and why someone else is suddenly stationed on Guam. If you decide to go, see if you can find out when I'm going to get my promotion to full colonel."

Libbie intertwined her fingers with Cole's. This trip had turned out to be so different from what she'd anticipated. It was supposed to be a time for them to see whether there was any possibility of meshing their lives, and she'd looked forward to coming to Washington, sure love would find a way. Instead, the problems of coping with Lai and the demands of Cole's assignment at the Pentagon had pushed Libbie's goals to the background. She was so busy seeing to everyone else's needs that her own identity seemed to be slipping away.

Would it be like this if she and Cole got married? What was happening to them? Always before, they'd met as equals, each giving due respect to the other's purposes and priorities. Now, in one short week, she was already becoming a nonentity. She'd have to go to the bridge party this afternoon and see whether she could be Cole's wife and still be her own person. There was a prickly feeling in her middle, and she hoped it wasn't a premonition that something was going wrong.

She lifted troubled eyes to Cole. "Does it seem to you that it's been a lifetime since we spent your leave at the lodge on Cat Mountain?" she asked. They'd been so happy then, so sure of their love.

"At least a lifetime," Cole answered, squeezing her fingers. "I'm sorry this trip has been such a disappointment to you."

"It's not a disappointment," she insisted. "It's just different."

"You can say that again." Cole tried to grin and failed. "We've gone from making love morning, noon, and night to never making love at all. I lie on the couch in the living room every night wishing I could sneak down the hall and crawl into bed with you. Hell, I haven't even gotten to give you a decent kiss."

"So you've noticed that, too?" Libbie said, stroking his palm with her long fingernails. At least he was giving her his undivided attention for the first time since she'd arrived. Maybe things would get back to normal and these doubts would go away.

Cole cocked his head to listen. The hair dryer was still whirring in the bathroom. "Thank God Lai's never cut her hair and it takes a long time to dry." He got to his feet and led Libbie down the hall into the living room, looking for the most private spot in the room. "Here," he said, opening the coat closet and drawing her inside, his hands already exploring her soft curves. "It's not much, but it's home."

* * *

Libbie took great pains with her dress and makeup for the afternoon bridge club, knowing she would be subjected to close scrutiny. She'd brought along a smart two-piece black dress, its sleeves puffed at the shoulder and tight along the arms, and its waist cinched with a wide belt and flaring out with a peplum. With black stockings and high-heeled shoes, she looked sophisticated enough for the nation's capital, though she felt like a small-town bumpkin. The insecurity about herself that was never far from the surface began to gnaw at Libbie, and by the time the taxi arrived for her, she was breathless from apprehension.

Don't get so flustered, she chided herself. You've never seen these women before and you may never see them again, so what's the big deal? Just act the way you did with Cole that night at the Pentagon ball. Smile, compliment them, smile again, and *move on*. She tried to swallow past a nervous lump in her throat. If only Cole were here with her, it wouldn't be so bad. He'd know how to act, and she could copy what he did.

The taxi pulled into the driveway of an attractive brick house, and by the time Libbie paid the driver, she was so agitated that she tipped him too much. She turned and looked down the long sidewalk. For a moment she thought about jumping in the taxi and going back to Cole's apartment. What on earth was she doing here, anyway? She was a peace activist. She didn't belong with a bunch of gossipy military wives.

"Is this the right address?" the taxi driver asked when she stood there without proceeding inside.

"Yes, it is. Thank you." She'd made her choice. The taxi drove away, and Libbie started down the walk.

"How nice to meet you," said her hostess at the door. "What a lovely dress you're wearing." Mrs. Jackson introduced Libbie to the woman beside her, and Libbie made her way down the line to the refreshment table. It wasn't so bad after all. She simply did exactly the same thing she'd done at the Pentagon, and it worked. She said as little as possible about herself, asked lots of questions about the interests of the people she met, and made small talk. It was all superficial, but it filled the time.

She thought she'd managed the occasion, until they were summoned to the room where bridge tables were set up. Once assigned to a particular foursome, it was impossible to dodge questions by moving about. The other women were good at the game of bridge and took it seriously enough that Libbie's frequent bidding blunders caused eyebrows to lift in irritation.

Don't judge me by my bridge game, Libbie thought defiantly. When it was her turn to be the dummy, everybody, including Libbie, was relieved. She left the table and found herself in a cluster of other women who were also sitting out the hand.

"I don't believe we've met," said a silver-haired woman in a stylish silk dress. "I'm Ginny DeWitt." She said the name as though Libbie should instantly recognize it.

"I'm Libbie Greer."

"Greer?" Mrs. DeWitt pondered the name. "Is your husband Captain Greer in the office of the secretary of the Air Force?"

"No, he isn't." For a moment Libbie thought she'd let the overbearing woman torment herself with a game of twenty questions, but she realized it would be ungracious. "I'm here as a guest," she explained. "I'm not an officer's wife."

"Oh, I see." Mrs. DeWitt obviously intended to find out whose guest Libbie was, and why. These bridge games were strictly for insiders.

"I'm a friend of Cole Matthews," Libbie said. "Perhaps you know him? He's with the Army."

"Lieutenant Colonel Matthews?" Mrs. DeWitt asked, emphasizing the rank. She gave Libbie a more careful appraisal. "My goodness, aren't you the lucky one?" she commented. "The city is full of women who've set their cap for our handsome colonel." Her tone conveyed, if her words did not, a definite message: *What's so special about you?*

Libbie did a slow burn. "How interesting," she said. "I've wondered myself how such a good-looking guy has stayed single all these years. I just don't understand why he'd take an interest in a small-town lobbyist like me."

Her sarcasm was lost on Mrs. DeWitt. "Lobbyist? You're a lobbyist?" She smiled eagerly at Libbie. "Let me guess," she insisted. "You must be with one of the defense contractors, but which one? You said a small town. Could it be one of the helicopter manufacturers? Or perhaps one of the data processing firms?" She paused so Libbie could give her an additional clue.

"No, ma'am. I'm not with the defense lobby." Libbie squared her jaw. "As a matter of fact, I'm a lobbyist with an antiwar activist group known as the Coalition for Nuclear Sanity. I've spent the last two years opposing the Pentagon."

Mrs. DeWitt gasped in surprise, and two other women turned to listen.

"I'm afraid I don't understand," Mrs. DeWitt said, ruffling her feathers. "If you're opposed to the Pentagon, then why are you here?"

Libbie lowered her voice to a conspiratorial whisper that could be heard by everyone at that end of the room. "That's a very good question," she said. "I certainly don't belong here, do I?" Libbie placed her cup and saucer on the tea table with a firmness that made them rattle. "If you'll give my regards to the hostess, I'll be on my way." With her head high, Libbie sailed from the room.

Chapter Twelve

The following day, Cole stowed Libbie's luggage in the trunk of his personal car, a brushed-silver Peugeot, and held the door for her while she settled herself on the pale gray leather upholstery. Lai had been sent to the movies and shopping at the mall with some of the girls she'd met at the circus yesterday. Cole had insisted that Lai make her own plans for the afternoon so he could take Libbie to National Airport for her return flight to Austin. Yesterday had been the disastrous finale to a week marked by trials. Everything was in a snarl, and maybe with some privacy, the two of them could think through their problems.

As Cole pulled the car into the Arlington traffic, he kept his eyes on the road, and Libbie turned to look out the window, chewing on her bottom lip to hold back the tears. Neither of them spoke, their minds on their dilemma.

This trip to Washington was a mistake, Libbie thought to herself. Our lives are on a collision course, and I might as well face that fact right now. It's time to pack away my dreams and accept reality. Libbie cringed, remembering the bridge party yesterday. How could she have let a foolish woman get her goat that way? She'd disgraced Cole, and possibly done harm to his career. Yet despite her juvenile behavior, which she regretted, she didn't fit in with the other women. Libbie couldn't give up her own personal goals and let herself be remade in the image of the proper officer's wife. If that was the price of marrying Cole, it was too high. She couldn't pay it.

There was plenty of time before they had to be at the airport, and Cole drove aimlessly for a while, taking roads that wound up into the hills with a view of the capital city below. They'd passed the Pentagon early in their drive, but neither of them made any comment. The building loomed as a five-sided concrete symbol of all the things that separated them.

Eventually Cole took Memorial Bridge across the Potomac and the Lincoln Memorial appeared directly in their path. It hurt them both too much to look at the statue of Lincoln and be reminded of that other time when they'd first acknowledged their love. They averted their eyes and stared back across the river.

By chance a car pulled out of a parking spot on the western edge of the Tidal Basin, and on impulse, Cole pulled into the space and turned off the car engine. The mass of Japanese cherry trees that bordered the Tidal Basin had been in riotous bloom two weeks earlier, drawing huge crowds, but the blossoms had now faded.

"The cherry trees blossomed early this year," Cole said. "I wish you could have seen them when they were in full bloom."

Libbie leaned back in the seat and gazed across at the trees, their tiny green leaves just emerging from a winter's sleep. "I guess the cherry trees are like us," she said in a choked voice. "Impatient and eager for our love to burst into full bloom, and then suddenly it's over."

"Is it over?"

She huddled her body into a ball and nodded.

Cole swore under his breath. "Libbie, what happened yesterday will blow over in a week's time. Everybody knows Mrs. DeWitt is a pompous ass, just like her husband."

"It isn't just her, Cole. It's everything. Lai hates me, the officers' wives expect me to be like them, I wouldn't be able to keep up my work for world peace, your job takes all your time—"

"Whoa, now," he said. "Let's take it one thing at a time. I never expected you to give up your work. I know how important it is to you."

"Be realistic, Cole. Everything I did would have an impact on your career. You'd never get your promotion to full colonel."

"I'm willing to take that chance." He reached for her hand. "I love you, Libbie. I want us to work things out."

She wiped away a tear that trickled down her cheek. "Sure, so do I," she answered. "And I want the lion to lie down with the lamb, and all the swords to be beaten into plowshares, and Lai to love me, and the cherry trees to blossom all year long." She drew a shaky breath. "What we want is impossible, Cole. It's never going to work."

Cole gripped the steering wheel with his left hand, and Libbie could see the muscle twitch at the corner of his jaw. "What's really eating at you, Libbie? We've got a lot of problems, sure, but you don't even want to talk about working them out. I thought you were a fighter. Why are you giving up on *us*, for God's sake? You never give up on anything else."

Libbie wished there were someplace to run. All the vague fears that had lain just below the surface were threatening to break loose. The ancient heartaches and failures that she'd tried to bury chose this moment to rise like ghosts to haunt her. "I'm the wrong woman for you, Cole. There's no room in your life for a person like me. I'd have to change too much, and every day I'd be wondering whether I'd changed enough to keep your love." She turned her head and looked out the side window. "I can't do it, not again. I have to be myself."

Cole gripped her shoulder and forced her head around so she had to look into the fiery depths of his eyes. "What do you mean you can't do it *again*?" he demanded.

"I don't want to talk about it." She tried to jerk her head away, but his fingers caught her cheek and held it fast.

"I don't give a damn whether you want to talk about it or not, Libbie. You're going to tell me, so let's have it."

She choked back tears, determined not to cry. "It was a long time ago, when I was in my first year of college," she said in a muffled voice. "I fell in love with a boy from a wealthy family, and he fell in love with me. We were going to get married, so he took me to meet his family in San Francisco. They were from one of the old, established families and lived in a mansion. There I was, a middle-class girl. I didn't have the right clothes or the right orthodontist. I didn't know how to act with all those servants and fancy socialite parties. I tried to fit in, but I was more comfortable with the gardener than I was with my boyfriend's family.''

"Did they snub you?'' asked Cole, trying to visualize Libbie as a young girl.

"Oh, no. They were much too well-bred for that. They couldn't have been nicer to me. His mother tried to help me by buying clothes for me and giving me suggestions on makeup. Every time I went there, they changed me a little bit more. But it was never quite enough.'' Cole's grip on her cheek loosened and she turned her head. She couldn't look him in the eye while she told the end of her story. "Then one day he told me he'd been mistaken and didn't love me after all. He'd decided to marry someone from his own social circle. That's when I gave up my scholarship at Stanford and came to Texas. I guess it's why I never wanted to go back to California.''

Cole pulled Libbie into his arms and sheltered her against his chest, stroking her hair while he murmured in her ear. "Is your opinion of me so low that you think I'd do the same thing?'' he asked.

Libbie straightened in Cole's arms and met his gaze head-on. "Cole, don't you understand?'' she asked in a plaintive voice. "What he did was *right*. I didn't fit into his life. I couldn't change enough to be the right person for him, and yet I couldn't be myself, either. I would've been miserable if we'd gotten married.''

Something within Cole closed in upon itself, and she felt him detach himself emotionally. When he spoke, his voice was full of an icy aloofness. "So you think you'd be miserable if you married me?"

"I think we'd work at it, and try hard, but I'd never be able to change enough for you, and someday you'd realize you didn't love me anymore. And yes, I'd be miserable, because every day of our marriage I'd be wondering if that would be the day you'd stop loving me."

There was a long, bitter silence.

"I've seen that insecurity in you," Cole said at last. "It's popped up at the strangest times, like the night we went to the Pentagon ball and the day you made your presentation to the congressional committee. I didn't understand it, because everything you did was sensational and brought you all kinds of compliments. You had every reason to be self-confident, but you weren't. Now it begins to make sense. What makes me mad as hell is that you don't have any confidence in *me*, either. When I say I love you, it's something you can count on. I'm not the kind of man to trifle with your heart, Libbie."

At the moment Libbie almost hated Cole for probing too deeply and exposing the core of her being, the hurting part that was hers alone. She lashed out at him. "I thought you trifled with everyone's heart," she said with heavy sarcasm. "Lady-killer Matthews, the Pentagon's secret weapon."

"Where did you hear a story like that?"

"From Jill. She told me how you kissed her in the moonlight and tried to seduce her."

Cole let out a string of profanity that was the jungle fighter's stock in trade.

"Do you deny it?" Libbie asked, almost intimidated by his reaction.

"I have absolutely no comment about anything that happened between Jill Wagner and me." Cole reached for the key and jerked it in the ignition so hard the metal grated. "It's time to go to the airport. You'd better check your luggage and see if you remembered to pack all the trash from the past you've been hauling around with you."

Libbie returned to her job at the Coalition in Austin and was almost immediately caught up in planning for a new meeting. A delegation of concerned citizens from the Texas Panhandle had requested an informal training session to give them ideas on things they could be doing as private individuals.

"They want one of us to fly up to the Panhandle," Libbie said, handing the letter to Jill. "They've recruited some new workers, and they want to get everybody organized for the rally at the Pantex facility in August."

"Did they send a check for expenses?" Jill asked, scanning the letter.

Libbie shook her head. "It may be hard to recruit workers, but it's even harder to get contributions. It doesn't sound like they have an operating budget."

Jill uttered a disgusted snort. "Neither do we. Our board is meeting soon to decide what to do about the Coalition. We're down to our last month's rent ourselves. We couldn't buy a box of envelopes right now, let alone pay for a trip to the Panhandle." She tossed aside the letter. "Tell them we're not in a position to help them at this time. Maybe we can go in a month or two, if a miracle happens and we find ourselves solvent."

Libbie read the letter again, with its plea for help. A peace vigil would be held outside the Pantex plant this coming August to commemorate the bombing of Hiroshima and Nagasaki. Pantex had been selected as the site because it was the final assembly point for all nuclear weapons produced in the United States. Plans would have to be made to feed and shelter a large group of people in an area along a strip of open highway miles from water and toilet facilities. The logistics of such an undertaking required hundreds of skilled workers. Someone had to take a group of inexperienced volunteers and whip them into a trained army.

"What if I drove my own car up there?" Libbie asked, trying to find a way to meet the request. "I might be able to stay with Molly Barnett or some of the other people we've gotten to know. That way it wouldn't cost the Coalition any money."

"Suit yourself," Jill said. "I don't know how you can afford to buy gasoline for your car, though, the way the board has cut our salaries."

Libbie's brows knotted in a troubled expression. "I'll manage," she said. "Even if I have to get a part-time job at the library or somewhere." Maybe it was just as well she was having to worry over financial difficulties. It helped to keep her mind off Cole Matthews and the gaping hole his absence had left in her heart.

Libbie drove to the Panhandle two weeks later and met with her group of volunteers in the auditorium of a small rural school. In the endearing tradition of West

Texas hospitality, they'd brought an abundance of covered dishes and made a festive social occasion of the training session. She was gratified to find an outpouring of enthusiasm and energy and felt optimistic that by August the group would be performing like veterans.

During the morning coffee break, Libbie had a chance to talk with Dan Williamson, whom she hadn't seen since November, when she and Cole had visited his farm.

"Too bad Colonel Matthews isn't here," Dan said with a grin that cracked his leathery face. "The missus sent *two* of her chocolate fudge cakes."

His words made Libbie twinge, reminding her as they did of Cole's boyish delight in rich desserts. "He certainly has a sweet tooth, doesn't he?" she replied, trying to smile.

"Yes, ma'am, he sure does. Tickled my wife pink, it did, to have him brag on her cooking that way. She told all the neighbors about him wrapping up a piece of her chocolate cake to take back to Washington with him."

Libbie glanced toward the long buffet table that had been set up in the cafeteria, searching for the high layered cake with its thick chocolate frosting. Maybe she ought to have a bite of it for old-times' sake. "I'd better get in line," she said, "or it's all going to be gone."

Dan joined her in the line and handed her a plate and fork. "That Colonel Matthews, he's quite a fellow," Dan said. "But I guess you noticed that for yourself." His knowing grin told Libbie that he hadn't missed the attraction that had sizzled between Cole and her that day.

She felt her cheeks redden. "You have to expect the Pentagon to send someone who has a way with people to do a job like this," she murmured.

"Oh, yes, ma'am, but he has something to him. You know what I mean? He's not just one of those drummers out to make a sale." Dan paused, recalling his judgment of Cole. "Ladies might get their hearts to fluttering over him, the way my missus did when he bragged on her. But a man can size up another man a lot better than a woman can. A man can tell Colonel Matthews is someone to count on when the chips are down."

Libbie's hand moved to her throat, instinctively trying to ease the lump that had risen there. "He must've made a good impression on you," she said.

"Yes, ma'am. I haven't been wrong too many times when it came to judging cattle or judging men. I'd say that boy is a square shooter all the way." They reached the chocolate cake and he cut a big wedge for Libbie. "I guess you heard about what he did."

Libbie gave him a perplexed look. "I'm afraid I don't know what you mean," she replied.

"Why, he's the one that got them to redo all those scientific tests and come up with some new safety features. I got a letter from the Pentagon here a few weeks back. Thanked me for going to Austin to express my concerns and said they'd found some new ways to protect our water supply and agriculture."

"I knew they'd ordered some additional tests," Libbie said, puzzling over this new information. "We didn't get any details about it, though."

"You didn't get one of those letters?" Dan was surprised. "That's odd. The letter said Colonel Matthews had initiated the study because of things you and your Coalition brought out at the hearings.''

Libbie had to discipline her mind not to mull over the things Dan had told her about Cole and instead concentrate on the training session at hand. She devoted the next portion of the meeting to teaching the volunteers how to set up a management time line, with deadlines for each separate task required by the peace vigil. Estimates were made in regard to the amount of food that would be necessary, the number of portable toilets, and the quantity of tents and other temporary shelters. Workers would also need to contact local law enforcement authorities in case a license was necessary, as well as assure the sheriff that the demonstration was intended to be peaceful.

The various activities were then divided and assigned to specific individuals, and soon each volunteer had a pretty good idea what his responsibility would be. By describing the rally in its entirety before breaking it down into its components, Libbie helped the volunteers see how each separate task was vital to the success of the entire operation. They began to feel a sense of pride in themselves and the importance of their role, the first step in creating the esprit de corps so essential to victory.

When they stopped for lunch, the excitement was beginning to build. Libbie sat at a table with some of the original volunteers, people she'd been working with for months, and gave them ideas on how to keep morale high over the next three months. Today was only the beginning, and the enthusiasm that sparkled now would need to be nurtured so it wouldn't fizzle out. When the afternoon session started, she knew it was time for her to step to the background and let the local leadership take over. They'd gained enough confidence to run their own show.

Molly Barnett, who'd once been so timid the words had had to be almost forcibly extracted from her, became one of the most stout-hearted members of the group. The loss of her son had given her a cause worth fighting for, and she inspired others to rally with her. She was flushed with a sense of accomplishment as she spoke to the group.

"We can make a difference," Molly insisted as she spoke into the microphone with a voice that was firm and clear. "I know that from my own personal experience. You all know how I went down to Austin last fall and told about the way my boy had been killed in an explosion at a weapons plant. I didn't want to go, but Libbie here, she talked me into it."

Molly turned to Libbie with a smile that gave her full credit for the transformation that had taken place, then continued. "I had a phone call a few weeks ago from an officer at the Pentagon. He said the Pentagon had listened to what I'd had to say that day in Austin, and ever since they've been going to weapons facilities and finding ways to improve the safety procedures. He said the Pentagon is going all-out to be sure no other mother loses her son in a senseless explosion that could be prevented."

Molly flung out her arms as though to draw everyone together in a common cause. "We're important," she said. "We can make things different. It doesn't matter if we're ordinary people from little towns nobody ever heard of. If we keep talking, we can make them listen, and if they listen, things will change. All we have to do is believe in ourselves and keep on fighting."

It was all Libbie could do to keep from rushing to Molly afterward and asking a thousand questions. Instead she tried to be casual. Fortunately Molly was more than eager to talk about the phone call she'd had from Cole, and the story bubbled from her lips.

"I could tell you were surprised," Molly said. "I figured you already knew, or I would've told you sooner. The colonel said you're the one that made him come up here to the Panhandle and see what was going on with his own eyes instead of relying on a bunch of written reports. He said he saw some things when he made an inspection, so he sent a team of experts out here and they drew up some new safety guidelines. Now they're going all over the country checking other places. He says it's going to take a long time to cover them all, because there are so many different facilities, but every month they make a little progress."

There was a funny little lilt in Libbie's heart. "Colonel Matthews talked about me?" she asked. At the moment, it was the most important information Molly had to share. Any sense of accomplishment over the new safety program was strictly secondary.

"Why, yes. He gave you all the credit. He said you'd made such a challenge to their safety procedures that they finally had to take another look." Molly reached for Libbie's arm. "It's warm in here, isn't it? I notice your face is as red as mine is. Let's get us a glass of iced tea and cool off."

Libbie returned to Austin with her mind in such a turmoil it was hard to untangle her feelings. She had a heavy sense of guilt every time she thought of how she'd acted at the bridge party in Washington. She'd put on a childish exhibition of temper and caused embarrassment to Cole, perhaps even hindered his Army career. Cole, however, had shown the utmost respect for her professional abilities and enhanced her prestige by giving her public credit for her success. He'd given better than he'd gotten in exchange, and Libbie winced to think how she'd shortchanged him.

She was also stunned to realize that there were depths to Cole she'd never imagined. She'd characterized him as a myopic militarist with a tilted view of the world, incapable of seeing anything except his own single-minded objectives. Instead, he'd listened with an open mind to every idea she'd presented, heard with a sensitive heart every human concern, and acted to make changes where they were needed.

Libbie felt a greater sense of loss than ever. She'd spent these past weeks convincing herself that she'd done the right thing, that there was no room in Cole's life for her, no hope to maintain her own identity with him—and she was right; she knew she was right. But, oh, how it hurt, being right. Why does it have to be this way? she raged inside herself. Why did I have to meet the right man at the wrong time? Why couldn't we have met before all these things happened to make our personalities the way they are now? Maybe if we'd met before, we'd have been young and inexperienced enough to want the same things out of life. Maybe we would've been able to work for the same goals instead of being on a collision course the way we are now. Maybe—

But it was no use trying to delude herself. Their personalities and characters were fixed, set in concrete, the result of all their life experiences. History couldn't be erased, and the past couldn't be changed. They had no future.

Bitterness rose in her like bile, and she went back to work in a foul mood.

"What's the matter with you?" Jill asked when Libbie had snapped at her for the third time that morning. "Did that long drive wear you out?"

"I guess so. I got a late start yesterday morning and didn't get home till late last night. Molly Barnett insisted on cooking a big breakfast before I left, and then we drank coffee and talked too long."

"Do you think the volunteers up there are going to be able to handle the August peace vigil by themselves?" Jill asked. There seemed to be tension in her voice, but Libbie was too preoccupied with her misery to pay much attention to it.

"I think so, if we can give them a little direction from time to time." Libbie walked to the window and looked out at the shiny green leaves of the azalea bushes. The azaleas had been so lovely when they'd bloomed, about the time she'd returned from Washington. Now all the bright pink and fuchsia flowers were gone, just like the blooms on the Japanese cherry trees in Washington. Just like the bloom had been blasted from life itself. She pushed her hair back from her face and wished the day were over. It was Friday, and she wanted the weekend to come so she could crawl into her lair like a wounded animal. She hadn't been so depressed in years.

"Libbie, I don't think you heard me," Jill said, her tone a little sharp.

"Sorry, I guess I was daydreaming. What did you say?"

"That we aren't going to be able to provide any direction to the volunteers in the Panhandle."

Libbie slumped against the windowsill and shook her head. "No, please don't say what I think you're going to say."

Jill nodded. "It's true. The board met on Wednesday while you were in the Panhandle. They voted to shut down the Coalition at the end of the month. We're broke."

"But, Jill, who's going to carry on our projects?" Libbie had refused to accept the possibility that this might happen, though Jill had tried several times to warn her. The work was so important that Libbie thought somehow they'd get the financial miracle they needed to keep operating.

"Our ongoing projects will be picked up by the Houston group. They'll wind things down, and of course there won't be any new projects started."

"I can't believe this." Libbie sat down and fought to keep from bursting into tears. "This is my whole life. What am I going to do?"

"I was on the phone all day yesterday," Jill said, her own expression as bleak as Libbie's. "I thought I could scramble and get good jobs for us, but things are really tight. It seems that lobbyists for activist causes aren't in much demand these days." She sighed. "There's a job with an agricultural group here in Austin. They'd like to talk with you about lobbying for them. They heard a lot of good things about the way you worked for the farmers in the Panhandle on the nuclear project, and they'll make a job for you."

"Doing what?" Libbie asked, her words fading away on a high-pitched note.

"Lobbying the Legislature for things that worry farmers," Jill answered. "Export quotas, price supports, agriculture loans, stuff like that."

Libbie's fists clenched. "That's not what I want to do," she said. "I know those things are important, but the first priority for my life is world peace. That's the cause I want to work for."

"Something will turn up eventually," Jill said, trying to reassure Libbie. "It's going to take a little time. For now, the job with the agriculture lobby will pay you a lot more than you're making here, and you'll be the senior staff member. If you can keep an open mind, it's really a promotion for you."

Libbie felt sick inside. She needed time to think. "What are you going to do?" she asked Jill. With her experience and reputation, Jill should be able to get her pick of jobs.

"I'm not sure," Jill said. "There's a part-time job in Houston with an antinuclear group, but the pay is terrible. It would mean trying to find another part-time job to survive, because it costs more to live in Houston than it does here. The Sierra Club may have something in California or Colorado if I can wait a few weeks."

"You mean you're going to move away from Austin?" Libbie said in surprise. They were both fond of their adopted city, which was really an overgrown small town with Southern charm and California casualness. "Why don't you take the job with the agriculture lobby here instead of letting me have it?"

"I think it's time for a change," Jill said. "I'm feeling restless."

"Maybe that's what's the matter with me, too."

For the first time Jill managed a genuine smile. "I think your restlessness is the kind that has to do with a man," she said. "Cole Matthews, to be precise."

"He's part of it. Not that it matters. There's no future in it."

"Yeah, that's the way he operates." Jill tossed a paper clip in the air and caught it when it came down. "What do they say, love 'em and leave 'em? That's Cole Matthews, all right."

It was too much. Usually good-natured, Libbie sometimes got angry, but she never lost her temper. Never. Today, to Jill's amazement, she did. "Why are you always on Cole's back?" Libbie said, her voice rising. "You're always making insinuations about him. What's he done that makes you cut him down?" The burning in Libbie's cheeks didn't compare with the fire that blazed from her eyes.

"I've told you before," Jill said, taken aback. "He tried to seduce me so he could find out what the Coalition's plans were." She lowered her voice, as though it might calm Libbie before she became hysterical.

It didn't work.

"I don't believe you!" Libbie cried. "He isn't like that!"

"Why don't you ask him about it, then, if you don't believe me?"

"I did. He wouldn't tell me."

Jill leaned back, her face puzzled. Then, as though laughter might defuse the emotional explosion that seemed imminent, she said, "It's going to be a real blow to my ego if he doesn't remember."

Even in her anger, Libbie managed a shaky giggle. "I think he remembers. It made him mad when I asked about it."

"Look, Libbie, we're adults. It was no big deal. I was in Washington a couple of years ago working on some project, and Cole was the Pentagon contact person. We hit it off, and one thing kind of led to another. When I realized he was trying to get information from me, I backed off."

Libbie pounded the desk with her fist. "He isn't like that," she insisted. "He never tried to find out anything from me. I don't understand it." Her eyes filled with tears.

"You really love the guy, don't you?" Jill said. "I never realized that before."

"I love him. We just don't have any future together, that's all."

Jill crossed her arms and chewed on a fingernail. "Well, future or not, there's no sense in your eating your heart out over the past. I wish I'd realized you were in love with him sooner, Libbie. I thought you were enjoying the game with him."

Libbie lifted her eyes to Jill's, then reached in her pocket for a tissue and blew her nose. "I did enjoy the game, but there was more to it than that."

"So I see." Jill took a deep breath. "Well, Libbie, if I weren't so fond of you, I wouldn't tell you this. It makes me look pretty bad. But I think I owe it to you to tell you the whole truth." She hesitated, then added, "I owe it to Cole, too. He was too much of a gentleman to tell you what I'd done. I wanted information from Cole, just like he wanted information from me. I set out to seduce him, but he was the one who backed off when he figured out what I was doing."

"Then why did you tell me it was the other way around?"

"That's the part I feel so bad about now," Jill answered, rolling her chair around to face the wall so she wouldn't have to look at the hurt in Libbie's eyes. "I wanted you to try to get information from him, and I knew you wouldn't do it unless you thought he was a manipulator, too. Sometimes you're just too wholesome and sincere to be a lobbyist."

"Did anybody ever tell you you're a cynic?" Libbie asked. She was angry and disappointed with Jill, but for now those feelings didn't count. What mattered was knowing her instincts about Cole were right. He was as honorable as she'd always believed. And he was honor bound to pursue his own course, charted in the opposite direction from hers.

Chapter Thirteen

Cole's head bent over his desk while he drafted a letter with firm, heavy strokes of his ballpoint pen. When he finished, he ripped the page from its pad and walked into the secretarial station that adjoined his office at the Pentagon. "I'd like to have this typed as soon as possible," he said to the efficient secretary who did most of the work for his department.

"Right away, sir," she said, putting aside the project she was working on.

While he waited, he walked down the hall to the coffee pot and poured himself a cup of scalding black coffee, then rummaged around till he found a doughnut left over from the previous morning. It was stale, so he dunked it in his coffee on the way back to his office.

He leaned back in his swivel chair and stared at the ceiling. God, it had been such a long month since Libbie had left Washington. They'd parted in anger, but after she was gone, his anger had quickly disappeared, to be replaced with a deep yearning of the heart. He'd missed her more than he'd ever have thought possible. Every minute was haunted by the memory of her warm smile, the merry ripple of her laughter, the soft tenderness in her eyes. Cole felt as though their separate lives had merged into one, the way two streams flow into a single river so that it's impossible to tell which drops of water belong to which stream. She'd gone away, and he was no longer whole.

As he'd predicted, the bridge party fracas was soon forgotten, at least by the wives who'd witnessed Libbie's moment of indignation. Cole, though, found his mind dwelling on the incident because of what it had revealed about Libbie's personality. It seemed incredible that a woman so beautiful and so capable could feel herself threatened by that kind of social situation. The disapproval of her fiancé and his wealthy family must have scarred Libbie for life. It touched Cole to think of Libbie as a vulnerable young girl, so eager to please, so willing to change. How it must have hurt her to be rejected despite all her efforts to gain their approval. No wonder she had lashed out at Mrs. DeWitt. No wonder she had refused to surrender her identity. No wonder she had refused a marriage with Cole that she thought would require her to mold herself into someone else's expectations.

But she was mistaken. Cole didn't want her to change. He loved her the way she was. And he couldn't live without her.

"Here's your letter, Colonel," said his secretary, her eyes studying his and then quickly glancing away.

"Thank you," Cole replied, taking it from her hand. "I'll be in Colonel Jackson's office." He finished his coffee and tossed his doughnut in the wastebasket, then walked down the hall. "Do you have a minute, sir?" he asked.

"Come in, Cole. Beautiful day, isn't it?" Colonel Jackson was looking out his window at the May-bright world. "After three years with Ho Chi Minh, I just never seem to get enough sunshine in these old bones of mine." He stretched, then sat down behind his desk. "You look like you've got something on your mind," he said. "What can I do for you, son?"

Without saying anything, Cole handed him the letter.

Colonel Jackson scanned the half-dozen lines, then lifted his head. "So you've decided to retire?" he said quietly.

"Yes, sir."

"I don't suppose that Texas gal has anything to do with this, does she?"

"She doesn't know about it, if that's what you mean." Cole met his commanding officer's direct gaze.

"Have you made any plans for your future?" the colonel asked, reaching for a cigarette. It would be his last one for the day, the one he usually saved for after dinner.

Cole shook his head. "Not really. First I've got to talk Libbie into marrying me. She's afraid she'll have to give up her work in the peace movement, so I've got to get that part of it straightened out before we can make plans."

"What about you, son?" The colonel took a deep drag of tobacco, then slowly exhaled. "Are you going to give up your own work? Seems to me that's going to be pretty hard for a man as dedicated as you are."

"Not as hard as giving up Libbie would be." Cole's fist clenched and unclenched. "I don't want to let her get away, Colonel. I've looked at it from every angle, and it comes down to this: I've had twenty years to fight for my cause. She's just getting started. She deserves her chance, just like I had mine. I can't hold her back. It wouldn't be fair." Cole felt his Adam's apple tighten. This was turning out to be harder than he'd bargained on. Giving up the Army was giving up a big part of himself.

"You know, Cole, I told you the Army was more flexible than you realized. I've been doing a little reconnaissance, because I had an idea you were going to decide to get married." The colonel gave Cole a tight-lipped smile. "I've talked to the general about what we might do with you if you wound up with a wife who wanted to carry a picket sign."

Cole grinned. "I don't think there's much question about that, sir. Right now all I can hope is that she doesn't put my picture on it."

"The general thinks that with *Challenger* going down and this Chernobyl meltdown, we need a new safety section in the Pentagon. If everybody's going to get on the safety bandwagon, the general thinks the

Pentagon might as well be at the front of the parade.''

"What do you mean, sir?" The conversation wasn't going at all the way Cole had anticipated.

"We think you're the man to put in charge of the new division. You've done an outstanding job of checking out some of these weapons facilities for safety improvements that can be made. We thought we'd put you to doing that full-time. No more trips to Paris." The colonel shuddered. "Isn't that the most miserable city in the world when it's cold and rainy?"

"But, sir—"

"Now, you'll still have to do some traveling, Cole. There's no way to avoid that. You'll be a trouble-shooter, and you'll have to visit these facilities from time to time. But the travel will all be stateside, and you'll spend most of your time here, at the Pentagon, directing a team of scientists and engineers. You can have fairly normal hours, and you'll still be doing an important job in the battle against oppression." The colonel took the last drag of his cigarette and regretfully stubbed it out. "Best of all, you'll still be making good use of your top-secret security clearance and the knowledge and experience you've spent twenty years accumulating. How about it, son? Shall I tear up this letter?"

"Colonel, I appreciate all you've done, but Libbie's work is in Austin. I don't think she's interested in coming to Washington to live."

Colonel Jackson's brow furrowed. "Didn't you see the letter that came through last week?"

"What letter?"

"That Coalition she worked for has shut down. They wrote and told us to direct all future correspondence to Houston because some outfit there is taking over the project."

"The Coalition has shut down?" A grin spread across Cole's face. "In that case, Colonel, tear up the letter. If you'll excuse me, I've got a few phone calls to make."

He started toward the door when Colonel Jackson's voice stopped him. "You've got one last trip to make, son. You're already briefed for the NATO meeting next week, and it's too late to prepare someone else. You'll have to go. The documents should be finished tomorrow afternoon. You'll leave for Paris the following morning."

Cole's head was whirring with ideas, and he paused in the doorway, trying to put things into a time sequence. "Will you do two things for me, sir?" he said when he'd sorted it out. "Will you give me thirty-six hours' leave so I can go to Oklahoma and talk to my daughter before I go to Paris?"

The colonel nodded. "What else?"

"With your permission, I'll take Libbie to Paris with me. Will you contact the American Embassy and see what we have to do to get married there?"

Colonel Jackson walked to the doorway and put a friendly arm across Cole's shoulder, offering his other hand for a congratulatory handshake. "You've got *my* permission, son. Now all you have to do is get *hers*."

Cole sat on the long, veranda-style front porch of his parents' ranch house outside Tulsa, Oklahoma, and talked to Lai while his mother was busy cooking supper. At first Lai had welcomed him and been unusually pleasant, but when he mentioned going to Paris, Lai began to sulk.

Cole stretched out his long legs and leaned back against the porch railing. Be patient but firm, he told himself. Remember what Libbie told you to do. Move in close and love Lai so much she won't be able to strike out. He took a deep breath and assumed a confidence he didn't feel. He pulled his daughter close to his side and hugged her. "Your mother would be very proud if she could see what a pretty girl you've turned out to be," he said.

"I don't even remember her," Lai said. "I was too little when she died."

"I'm sorry you can't remember her," Cole said softly. "She was a wonderful mother to you. She was so happy when you were born."

"I wish I had a picture of her. I don't even know what she looked like."

Cole sighed. "There aren't any pictures. Everything was destroyed when Saigon fell," he said. "We were lucky to get out with our lives."

"My mother wasn't so lucky."

"No, she wasn't. But she'd been very happy, Lai. You must always remember that. She had you and me to love, and even in the worst part of the war, she'd hold you close and smile at you with absolute joy on her face. She gave you a lifetime full of love in those two short years. A lot of people live to be eighty and never know as much happiness as your mother did in her brief lifetime."

"Were you happy when she was alive?"

Cole watched the shadows move across his daughter's lovely face. They'd never talked like this before, and for the first time he realized how Lai must have wondered about these things that he'd locked in silence. In protecting himself from pain, he'd created it in his child.

"Oh, yes." He cleared his throat. The grief that he'd never let himself express seemed determined to break from its hiding place. "We were very much in love, the way you're going to be someday. I hope you'll be as happy as we were, your mother and I."

"If you loved my mother so much, why do you want to marry Libbie?" Lai pouted, and all her jealousy spilled over. "Can't you be faithful to my mother's memory?"

Cole embraced her shoulders and held her tight against him. "Maybe you're too young to understand," he said gently "There's nothing about my love for Libbie that's disloyal to your mother. I think Nguyot would understand and be glad that I've finally found someone else. Libbie isn't going to take your mother's place in my heart. No one could ever do that. Libbie has her own place, just like you do."

Lai struggled and tried to break loose, but Cole held her fast.

"Lai, you wouldn't want a father with a heart so small he could never love but one person."

"Yes I would, if that person was me!" She buried her face against Cole's shoulder and began to cry. "All my life I've wanted you to love me, but you didn't. You always went off and left me. I begged you to take me with you, but you wouldn't. No matter how hard I tried, I couldn't make you love me enough to want me with you. And now you want Libbie, but you still don't care about me. I hate her!"

"Shh, baby, don't," Cole said, trying to comfort her while she squirmed and tried to wiggle out of his arms. "I do love you, Lai, believe me."

"No, you don't! If you loved me, you'd want me with you!"

Her anguish was unbearable. Cole felt his heart break, and he lifted Lai onto his lap and held her the way he had when she was a tiny baby. There was nothing he could say to counteract the truth she knew in her child-wise heart. He hadn't wanted her with him. He hadn't wanted to bother with her. But why? Had he kidded himself all these years when he'd said it was the demands of his work?

Cole rocked Lai in his arms while his inner defenses crumbled. He hadn't wanted his own child because he had nothing left to give her. For years he'd kept everyone else at bay, avoiding any kind of genuine relationship, because he was cold and dead inside without even realizing it. Then Libbie came along, with her brave, generous heart, and breathed new life into him and taught him how to love again. Because of Libbie, he could finally feel love for his own daughter. Cole's arms tightened about Lai's slender, delicate body and hugged her till she couldn't catch her breath.

"Daddy, you're squeezing me to death," she protested, but there was joy in her voice.

"I love you, baby," he said. "I love you so much."

Lai lifted her bright face to his and flung her arms around his neck. "Oh, Daddy, I love you, too!"

Cole reached in his hip pocket for a handkerchief so he could dry her eyes, then discovered that the wet tears on his cheeks were his own.

The evening breeze ruffled the leaves in the cottonwood trees, and Cole and his daughter sat on the porch steps until the sun went down. When his mother called them for supper, they went arm in arm into the house. Cole's father, in his sixties, still as straight and tall as Cole, with the same proud carriage, came in from the field where he'd been branding calves. Over supper, Cole told his parents about Libbie and his hope that she'd marry him.

"Haven't you asked her yet?" asked Mrs. Matthews.

"Not lately."

"When do you want to get married?" asked Cole's father.

"Day after tomorrow. In Paris"

There was an explosion of laughter around the table.

"Don't you think maybe you ought to find out how the lady feels about it?" Mr. Matthews passed a heaping platter of fried chicken for seconds, then laughed again.

"I wanted to talk to Lai first. I needed to see how she feels about it." Cole waited to see if Lai was going to turn hostile, but she seemed at peace now that she was sure of his love.

"Libbie's pretty neat," Lai said to her grandmother. "She took me around Washington and was as nice as could be, even when I acted like a brat." Lai grinned at her father, and he was amazed to see that it was a lopsided grin identical to his own, strangely right at home on her tiny Amerasian face. "Tell her I'll act better the next time, Daddy. I don't want to scare her off."

Cole reached across the table for Lai's hand. "After supper we'll call her and you can tell her yourself," he said. "If we're lucky, she'll fly to Tulsa in the morning and meet your grandma and grandpa."

The trip from the Tulsa airport to the Matthews ranch fifteen miles away took over an hour, because every five minutes or so Cole would pull his father's pickup truck to the side of the deserted dirt road and kiss Libbie until they were breathless.

"I can't believe you're really here," Cole said, stroking her cheekbones with his thumbs while he smiled down at her.

"I'm having a little trouble believing it myself," she answered, catching his wrist and holding it still while she nibbled at the fleshy mound at the base of his thumb. "We have a lot to talk about."

"First things first," he said. He took his eyes from Libbie's long enough to check to see whether another car had erred onto the private road. "It's safe," he said. "This is our family's road. No one will see us."

He pulled her so close to him she could feel the muscles tighten across his chest, and then he claimed her mouth, stroking it with his tongue until her lips trembled in response. Her heart began to thud rapidly, forcing the blood through her veins so fast there was a roaring in her ears. It was a delightful dizziness, and when he would have broken away, she pursued him with her lips, demanding more.

He groaned and let his hands slip to her waist, then up and around until he cupped the soft roundness of her breasts. His breathing quickened, and urgent moaning sounds rose from the back of his throat. Desperately he twisted her body in his arms to allow free access to her tempting curves and valleys. His hand slipped underneath her loose cotton bouclé top to free her breasts and quickly stroked and kneaded them to a tingling arousal. She whimpered with pleasure, and he lowered his head, searching for her nipple with lips that were warm and moist.

She arched against him, letting him draw more of her nipple into his mouth, then easing away to create a voluptuous stretching of her rosy, quivering bud. His tongue traced fiery circles, then closed with a greedy suction, as though he would draw forth her honeyed essence. He turned to work the same magic on her other breast, and a liquid warmth spread out from the center of her being. "Cole," she cried, feeling herself lifted in a wave of passion that was ready to crest and toss her high into the realm of utter sensation.

Libbie lay back on the seat, and Cole stretched himself over her, fumbling with their clothes until the love-eager parts of their bodies were bare and joined together in a torrid, thrusting ascension. Eager and ready, they kindled the fuse of their desire until it sparked and flamed, then burst like a rocket carrying them ever higher to a cataclysm of love....

Libbie tilted the rearview mirror and looked at her reflection. Her lips were slightly swollen and felt bruised, and her eyes had a sensual glow. "People will be able to tell what we've been doing," she said, blissfully contented.

Cole straightened her blouse over her breasts and smoothed away a wrinkle. He grinned when his touch made her nipple pucker all over again. "Don't you ever get enough?" he teased.

Libbie leaned her head against the seat and looked at him with dreamy eyes. "Do you?" she asked, opening her arms to embrace him.

They kissed, a light, gentle kiss.

"I always get a little frenzied when we're alone," Libbie said with a smile. "I'm afraid you'll get snatched away from me, so I have to get all of you I can while you're here."

Cole tilted her chin. "If you'll marry me, we won't ever have to be separated again," he said in a low voice. He looked as young and scared as a high school boy asking for his first date.

"Cole, please," Libbie said, turning her face to look out the window at the meadow grass and cottonwood trees. "We've been over this before. It won't work." A sigh trembled through her. "We'll have to make do with little bits and pieces of each other now and then."

"That's not enough for me, Libbie." Cole's voice steadied and grew firm. "I don't want an affair. I want a wife."

"You want someone who'll fit into your life as an Army officer. I'm not the one to do it."

"What if I told you I was prepared to change my life so you can be happy with me?"

Libbie was startled. "How?"

"First tell me if you love me."

Libbie lifted his fingers to her lips and kissed them. "You already know the answer to that," she said softly.

"I want to hear you say it."

Libbie lifted herself onto her knees and rubbed Cole's nose with hers, then kissed the corner of his mouth. "I love you with all my heart, Cole Matthews."

He pulled her onto his lap and accidentally hit the horn with his elbow, sending a loud honking sound across the peaceful countryside. "Do you hear that, Oklahoma?" he shouted. "Libbie loves this ol' soldier boy!" The smile he gave her was so full of happiness it brought tears to her eyes. "Come here, darlin'," Cole said, putting his arms around her, "and let me tell you all the plans I've made for us."

Libbie leaned across him and stuck her head out the window. "Do you hear that, Oklahoma? This ol' soldier boy hasn't changed a bit. He's still barking out orders." She dissolved in helpless laughter. "Cole, do you think you could *ask* me what I think of these plans you've made for us?"

He shook his head. "Nope. I've asked you three times to marry me, and every time you've said no. This time I'm telling you. Tomorrow we fly to Paris, and the day after that, we're getting married."

Libbie's heart began to pound wildly. "You're serious, aren't you?"

"You're damned right."

"Then we'd better be on our way to meet your family. We've got a lot to talk about with Lai."

"Just one more thing, sweetheart," Cole said. "We'll be staying with my mom and dad tonight." His ears turned red. "Mom's giving you my room and making a bed for me on the couch. You know how mothers are."

Libbie smiled and brushed her lips against his. "In that case," she whispered huskily, "maybe we'd better make the most of our privacy right now."

There was a radiance shimmering from Cole and Libbie that told Cole's parents their son had found real love. They took to Libbie at once, pleased at the transformation she'd brought about in Cole. As for Cole, he couldn't seem to let Libbie out of his sight, and his eyes clung to hers even as his hand unconsciously reached to touch her shoulder or slip around her waist. When he told his family about the work she'd been doing with the Coalition, there was pride in his voice. He loved her and wanted to show her off to the people who mattered most to him.

Lai stayed in the background, watching and trying not to feel jealous. Somehow she knew that Libbie was responsible for the change in Cole, and that made it easier for her to share him. Libbie wasn't so bad, Lai told herself. At least she talked to Lai as though she was a real person, instead of talking down to her, the way grown-ups usually did. Besides, from now on Libbie was going to be in Washington when Lai went to visit, so she might as well get used to the idea.

After lunch, Mrs. Matthews insisted on cleaning up the kitchen by herself. Mr. Matthews had gone back to the barn, and Cole and Libbie sat on the sofa holding hands. Lai sat on a window seat pretending to do her homework for Monday.

"Didn't I see a rope swing in the big cottonwood tree out in back?" Libbie asked.

Lai nodded. "Grandpa made it for me when I was a little girl."

"I've always loved rope swings," Libbie said. "Do you mind if I use it?"

Lai turned the page in her math book. "No, go ahead."

"Would you come with me?" Libbie asked. "I might need a push." She disengaged herself from Cole's arm and stood.

"I'll give you a push," Cole offered.

"You stay here," Libbie said in a voice too low for Lai to hear. "It's time for us to have a woman-to-woman talk." She walked over to the window seat and put an arm around Lai's shoulders. "I'd like your company," she said.

Lai looked at Cole, then back at Libbie. "Okay." She closed her book and followed Libbie out the side door.

They walked through the gate down to the gnarled old tree with its many large boughs. Libbie sat down on the piece of inner tube that had been cut to make a seat for the swing, and Lai sat down in the sweet-smelling grass at her feet.

"You don't really want to swing, do you?" Lai asked. Her tiny face was pinched and frightened.

Libbie shook her head. "I wanted us to have a chance to talk," she said softly, reaching for Lai's hand. "I know it must be hard for you to have your father get remarried."

Lai blinked back a tear. "It's okay with me," she said. "He deserves to be happy."

Libbie reached out to stroke Lai's cheek. "You deserve to be happy, too."

Lai shrugged. "I'm happy. Grandma and Grandpa are good to me, and I have my horse and cat."

"I guess most of your friends have a mother and a father, and maybe some brothers and sisters." Libbie studied Lai's face, so hauntingly beautiful, so terribly vulnerable. "That's not quite the same thing as a horse and a cat, is it?"

Lai reached down to pull a handful of grass from the dark, moist earth. There was a long silence.

"I'm going to get a job in Washington," Libbie said. "I think I'd like to work on a congressman's staff for a while."

"That sounds like it would be neat," Lai replied. "What would you be doing?"

"I'd still be working for world peace, but on the inside, instead of from the outside like I've been doing. I'd be researching proposed legislation and writing newsletters, things like that." Libbie pulled Lai's head onto her lap and stroked her thick black hair. "I think I'll work for a year or two and then stop and have a baby."

"Oh."

"I haven't told your dad yet." Libbie's laugh was lighthearted. "He'd say he's too old. I'll probably just surprise him."

Lai mumbled something Libbie didn't understand.

"Lai, look at me." Libbie waited until Lai lifted her face and their eyes met. "I know it makes you uncomfortable for me to talk about things like this. You've got to understand that your father and I are in love, and we're going to get married. We're going to share the kind of intimacy that comes with being married, and sooner or later it's going to lead to having a baby. You're old enough to know that."

"It doesn't mean I want to talk about it. It makes me feel weird to think of my own father doing stuff like that."

Libbie bit her lip to keep from laughing. She didn't want to make Lai feel any worse than she already did. "I want you to think about it anyway, Lai, and this is why. When you finish your school year in a few weeks, I'd like for you to come to Washington and live with us. Permanently."

Lai's hand flew to her throat. "Live with you?" she squealed.

"If you can handle the fact that your dad and I are going to be sleeping together, and sometimes we're going to kiss each other in the middle of the kitchen for no reason at all. I'm not willing to go hide in the closet every time we want to do a little smooching."

"But, Libbie, why would you want me to come live with you?" Lai asked in a mournful voice. "I was so hateful to you when we were in Washington last month. I wouldn't blame you if you hated me."

Libbie opened her arms and wrapped Lai in a circle of love. "I want you to live with us because I love your father. You're part of him, so you belong with us." After a moment, Libbie added, "Cole needs you, Lai."

"He doesn't need me." Lai's words were muffled against Libbie's shoulder. "He doesn't even want me."

"Yes, he does. He's just a little scared of you, that's all. He's afraid he can't give you what you need."

"Did he tell you that?"

Libbie shook her head. "No. He didn't have to tell me. I could figure it out for myself." She looked down at Lai and saw her face beaming with happiness. "What do you say, Lai? Shall we give it a try?"

Lai's arms stole around Libbie's neck, and she gave her a shy hug. "I guess I'm beginning to understand why Daddy loves you," she said.

Libbie sighed with relief. "I'm glad that's settled," she said. "Let's go in and tell your father." They walked back to the house with their arms around each other's waists. When they reached the porch, Libbie said, "Do you think you can afford to miss school for a few days? Maybe we can talk Cole into letting you go to Paris for the wedding. I'm going to need a maid of honor."

"Do you mean it?" Lai's tiny body was squirming with delight.

Libbie nodded. "You can go for the wedding. But when we get ready to start our honeymoon, you have to come back home."

Lai gave Libbie the grin that was so characteristic of Cole. "Who wants to go on a yukky old honeymoon?" she said, wrinkling her nose.

Cole had come to the door when he heard their voices. "I do," he said. "The yukkier, the better."

While Cole spent the day with the military attaché in Paris, Libbie and Lai risked their lives with French taxi drivers in order to shop to their hearts' content. Cole had given them carte blanche to buy anything they wanted. He assured them that most of his salary for the twenty years he'd been in the Army had been collecting in the bank, because he never had time to spend it.

Lai selected a bridesmaid's dress the pale yellow of meadow buttercups, its bodice smocked and its skirt full and flowing. Libbie found the perfect wedding dress of ivory Chantilly lace over a satin underslip of pale blue. Feeling totally extravagant, she went into a lingerie shop and bought a bridal nightgown and peignoir of sheer blue silk trimmed with wide bands of matching lace. It cost as much as she usually spent on clothes in two or three months, and she grinned wryly to think it was probably a waste of money. The lovely garments would probably remain in her suitcase during their entire honeymoon.

They bought several other dresses as well as shoes, costume jewelry, and delicate underwear, admiring each other's taste and sharing the fun of shopping when there was no need to consider the expense. By four o'clock they were exhausted and had so many packages, the back seat of the taxi was piled high.

"American Embassy," Libbie said to the driver, then put her hands over her eyes for the daredevil ride. She couldn't bear to watch.

The taxi careened to its destination, and the driver helped them with their parcels. They were met at the door by a gracious silver-haired woman in an elegant long gown. "Come in," she said. "I believe everything is ready for you." She showed Libbie and Lai to a guest room upstairs so they could bathe and change.

"It's so kind of you to help us," Libbie said. "It's really a terrible imposition for you to take charge of a stranger's wedding with no notice at all."

The ambassador's wife smiled at them. "It's been a lot of fun," she said. "Over the years I've done so many big formal receptions and seated dinners for a hundred guests. An elopement is something brand new for me."

"The Embassy is beautiful," Libbie said. "Our wedding will be like something in a storybook. I'm already beginning to feel like a princess."

"I've met Colonel Matthews before," the ambassador's wife said. "I must agree that he'd make any woman feel like royalty." She checked to be sure they had everything they needed. "Colonel Matthews will be here in an hour," she said, then started to the door so they could get ready. "The ambassador will be with him. Don't be surprised if he's a little nervous. He's never performed a wedding ceremony before."

Lai showered, then put on her dress and primped in front of the mirror. She knew she'd never looked so delicate or so pretty before. Surely her father would be just as proud of her as he was of Libbie.

Libbie took a leisurely soak in the tub, then dusted herself with good-smelling bath powder before donning her old bathrobe to do her makeup and hair. "Oh, Lai," she said when she came out of the bathroom. "You look lovely. You're the prettiest bridesmaid I've ever seen."

Lai did a graceful turn and came to give Libbie a hug. "Thank you."

There was a knock at the door.

"Hi, Daddy," Lai said, opening it for Cole.

He put his hands around her slender waist and lifted her in the air. "My goodness but you're beautiful," he said. He turned to Libbie, standing by the dresser in her old robe. "So are you," he said, walking over to Libbie.

"I actually think you mean that," Libbie said, giggling. "Even when I'm in my worn-out robe." She lifted her face and he kissed her lips. "Umm, that was nice," she said.

He started to kiss her again, then caught sight of Lai and stopped with a guilty expression on his face.

"Never mind me," Lai said with a wave of her hand. "I know you're going to do stuff like that sometimes." Her almond-shaped eyes were indulgent. "Grown-ups!" she said.

"Yeah, grown-ups," Cole said in a husky voice. He kissed Libbie again. "You've got thirty minutes to change your mind," he said.

"So do you," Libbie answered, leaning against his shoulder and luxuriating in the solid strength of it.

"I'll take my chances."

"Then so will I." Their eyes met and clung, sealing their promise with love.

Thirty minutes later, Libbie and Lai walked down the hallway and paused at the top of the spiral staircase. Someone began to play the wedding march on a piano, and Lai stepped forward, then went down the steps in the slow, graceful walk of a bridesmaid. When Lai reached the fifth step, Libbie began her descent on the arm of a military attaché, her eyes sparkling with light reflected from a crystal chandelier. Beyond Lai's slender body, Libbie could see Cole waiting for them at the foot of the stairs, dressed in his blue formal dress uniform. Her heart began to beat a little faster.

Lai took Libbie's bouquet of baby's breath and yellow roses, tied in a lace-trimmed nosegay with blue satin streamers, then stepped to one side. The military attaché stepped to the other side, leaving an open space. Cole offered his crooked elbow to Libbie, claiming her as his bride, and they turned to face the ambassador.

They made their vows with faces that were radiant with love, with voices that trembled with joy. "Do you promise to love, honor, and cherish this man so long as you both shall live?" asked the ambassador.

"I do," Libbie replied, smiling into the eyes of her beloved.

The ambassador lost his place and fumbled for the next line. Cole placed his arm around Libbie's waist, then beckoned to Lai. She came to stand on his other side, and he drew her into the circle with himself and Libbie. With a voice that was confident and full of hope, he ad-libbed his own personal vow: "I promise to forsake all others, resist all foes, and make this world a place of peace and safety for Libbie and our children—and for all the generations who come after us—forever and ever. Amen."

And then Libbie's soldier bent his head to kiss his bride.

Silhouette Special Edition

COMING NEXT MONTH

CRISTEN'S CHOICE—Ginna Gray
Finding a blatantly virile, nearly naked man in her bathroom gave Cristen the shock of her life. But Ryan O'Malley's surprises didn't stop there, and his teasing sensual tactics left her limp with longing—and perpetually perplexed!

PURPLE DIAMONDS—Jo Ann Algermissen
When beautiful heartbreaker Halley Twain was assigned to his ward, Dr. Mark Abraham knew she meant danger. After reopening his old emotional wounds, would she have the healing touch to save him?

WITH THIS RING—Pat Warren
Nick flipped over kooky Kate Stevens, but she was his brother's girlfriend, and the two men already had a score to settle. Still, Nick couldn't stop himself from wanting her.

RENEGADE SON—Lisa Jackson
With her farm in jeopardy, Dani would do anything to save it. But when sexy, rugged Chase McEnroe seemed determined to take it from her, she wondered just how far she'd have to go....

A MEASURE OF LOVE—Lindsay McKenna
Jessie had come to protect wild horses, but one look at proud, defiant rancher Rafe Kincaid was enough to warn her—it was her heart that was in danger.

HIGH SOCIETY—Lynda Trent
Their families had feuded for years, but mechanic Mike Barlow and socialite Sheila Danforth felt nothing but attraction. Could the heat of their kisses ever melt society's icy disdain?

AVAILABLE NOW:

FIRE AT DAWN
Linda Shaw

THE SHOWGIRL AND THE PROFESSOR
Phyllis Halldorson

HONORABLE INTENTIONS
Kate Meriwether

DANGER IN HIS ARMS
Patti Beckman

THEIR SONG UNENDING
Anna James

RETURN TO EDEN
Jeanne Stephens

FOUR UNIQUE SERIES
FOR EVERY WOMAN YOU ARE...

Silhouette Romance

Heartwarming romances that will make you
laugh and cry as they bring you all the wonder
and magic of falling in love.

6 titles
per month

Silhouette Special Edition

Expanded romances written with emotion and
heightened romantic tension to ensure
powerful stories. A rare blend of passion and
dramatic realism.

6 titles
per month

Silhouette Desire

Believable, sensuous, compelling—and
above all, romantic—these stories deliver
the promise of love, the guarantee
of satisfaction.

6 titles
per month

Silhouette Intimate Moments

Love stories that entice; longer, more
sensuous romances filled with adventure,
suspense, glamour and melodrama.

4 titles
per month

Silhouette Romances
not available in retail outlets in Canada

SIL-GEN-1A